KENNINGTON HOUSE MURDER

The Violet Carlyle Historical Mysteries

BETH BYERS

SUMMARY

April 1923.

After a visit to the Amalfi Coast, Lady Violet returns home
for her sister's wedding. When Vi meets her sister's fiancé,
she knows something must be done.Only, before she can stop
the wedding, someone else does.

This time, instead of being a suspect, Inspector Jack Wakefield knows she's innocent. He's not eyeing her for the crime,
but she's captured his attention.

Can they find the killer, so they can explore what's growing
between them? And just how will her family react when they
discover she's falling for a Scotland Yard detective?

Pam. Gurrrllll.

<3 you.!

CHAPTER ONE

"Ah," Violet said merrily, glancing up at her brother, "home sweet home."

The drizzle turned to a downpour, and she laughed as the boat rocked beneath their feet. Each of them were drenched through their clothes and would require hot baths and hot toddies at the earliest possible moment. The cliffs of Dover were in the distance but rather hard to make out with the rain —still...it was home.

"We're going to get horrifically ill. Sniffles for days." Victor glanced back towards the entrance to the cabins and then shuddered as he recalled what was happening in there. "How many stone do you think Gwennie is currently...expelling?"

Violet nudged her brother with an elbow and ignored the statement. Poor Gwennie got notoriously ill whenever they were in an automobile, train, or boat.

Violet gripped the railing and leaned down until Victor grabbed the back of her overcoat.

"After the Amalfi coast, the English Channel is something of a disappointment, isn't it?"

"Grey water, cold that seeps into your bones, and storm clouds? Yes, rather. I'd give buckets of money for a patio overlooking the sea and a cup of Turkish coffee."

The twins stood on the deck, holding onto the railing. The water was rough but not dangerously so. The cabin they'd taken was filled with the scent of sick, so they'd escaped to the wetter but fresher air. Without a regret, they'd left their friend Lila and the maid Beatrice to deal with the sick Gwennie, as both of them erred on the side of sympathetic illness.

When the two of them were side-by-side, they proclaimed their status as twins. They were both slim with dark hair, dark eyes, elfin faces, and clever expressions. Both of them had a merry and lively look to their eyes.

"I'm having rather a hard time imagining Isolde married," Violet confessed. "I know that's why we're going home, so I suppose it must be happening, mustn't it? I keep thinking of her when I first saw her. You remember. We'd had the measles, so we didn't meet Isolde until after she was several months old. Pink, chubby cheeks, that long white dress on her. The little bonnet. The scent of sour milk under her chins."

"Well," he said rather lightheartedly, "I had been having a rather hard time imagining her out of the school. It took me a bit to realize that last time I saw her she *was* in the schoolroom, and I've never yet met this grown-up version of our little sister."

Violet nudged her brother. The twins and Isolde didn't share a mother, and the two of them had spent rather a lot of time with the relatives on their mother's side while Isolde had done the opposite. In many ways, they were strangers.

"I feel like we're losing her before we've even gotten to

know her," Violet said. "Is it losing Aunt Agatha that makes me mourn Isolde in advance?"

Victor pressed a kiss to Violet's head and then said, "You lost two mothers, Vi, and not very much time has passed since the last one. Isolde isn't dying. She's just marrying. We'll see her again, and she'll present us little cherubic, double-chinned offspring to cluck over."

"Isolde is following the path Lady Eleanor laid out before she's even had a chance to form wants of her own. It's...sad." A concerned look crossed Violet's face before she added, "Do you think she really wants to be married? Could she, truly? She's within a breath of eighteen.

Surely this is all Lady Eleanor's engineering."

"Certainly, Lady Eleanor has a lot to do with this, Vi. You know our dear stepmother sees marriage as the moment when she can wash her hands of you. Perhaps it's the same for her own child." Victor let the smooth carelessness of his expression fade and continued, "Thinking of myself at Isolde's age, the idea of being married is...terrifying."

"Darling," Violet said, winding her arm through her brother's elbow, "the idea of strapping on the old ball and chain at your *current* age is terrifying. Admit it."

He grinned and winked at Violet before he said, "You know me too well, love. As for Isolde...do I believe that Lady Eleanor has pushed this sham of a marriage? Of course I do. Yet darling, I also think that Isolde won't hear our objections. She always was a romantic little thing, playing with baby dolls at the age you were racing to the swimming hole. It's better to let this one go. Perhaps, if we handle things just right, and she needs us later, she'll come our way."

Violet sighed and nodded and turned back to the ocean, placing her head on his shoulder.

She rather feared her brother was correct about Isolde's fate.

Docking at Dover was what one would expect. Busy, wet, and fraught with frustration. They gathered up a porter and their bags and determined to stay in a hotel before they caught the train to London. Gwennie was so green and frail looking they weren't quite sure her health wouldn't have been irreparably harmed by adding in yet another journey. And there was the lure of a hot bath and a hot drink, which sounded more important than getting to London before another day passed. They found rooms, baths, and hot drinks in that order.

It was only afterward that they thought of dinner. The hotel restaurant served an excellent roasted chicken dinner. After the luxurious Italian food they'd enjoyed for months, the familiar British roasted potatoes, veg, and chicken felt almost as much like coming home as the drizzle.

They all partook heavily, but Gwennie tucked in like a starving urchin.

"Darlings," Lila announced, raising her glass of wine, "thank you for the lovely time abroad. Here's to our own beds, seeing my love again, and a day where Gwennie isn't sicking up in the background."

Gwennie blushed brilliantly. Violet nudged her and said, "The woebegone lamb look is good for you, darling. Perhaps a certain Mr. Davies will be in London for business?"

"If so," Victor said, enjoying Gwennie's flush even more than Violet, "we should have a dinner party. I did buy rather a lot of spirits that need a party to be appreciated."

"What a wonderful idea, brother dear. You *are* a brainy one, aren't you? Well dear,"

Violet said to Gwennie, "shall we have a dinner party in the new home? Invite the dashing Mr.

Davies and perhaps our little lamb of a sister, winner of the race to the altar?"

"We do need to assess this future in-law," Victor said with

a shudder, adding, "Isolde is welcome to the prize of first to be married, though I should much rather see Gwennie in possession of that crown than our Isolde. Gwennie has the look of a pair of shackles one would wear happily. Whereas little sister is too fresh and new to be quite sure what kind of shackles she'll become."

"She is horribly spoiled," Violet sighed. "She might be a little too tight and needy."

"Unlike you," Victor teased.

Lila snorted. "Violet will be the shackles whose love will ever be trying to locate and put back on."

Gwennie laughed, all sign of illness gone except for the dark circles under her eyes.

"Ah...Violet, the elusive shackles."

"I am not shackles," Violet declared and then sniffed virtuously. "I am a prize."

"A pearl of great price," Victor called as he tapped off his cigarette.

"More valuable than rubies," Lila added, holding out her cigarette for Victor to light.

Violet scowled at both of them, waving the smoke out of her face. With a scrunched nose she said, "Oh! You spent rather too much time with missionaries on our boat."

"We couldn't all snuggle into the stateroom with a pile of French novels, darling," Victor said. "Do not disparage my friend, the fine brother Malachi. Not only was he a great imparter of the good word, he is quite an excellent gambler. I haven't had a series of games that hard-fought since Oxford."

Violet cast her brother an appalled look. "How much did you lose?"

"Enough to keep God's work rolling for a good long time," Lila laughed. "Sister Hannah objected at first until she saw how effectively Brother Malachi was pulling in the filthy lucre.

Then she snapped her mouth shut and watched with an avaricious gaze."

"One must support the good work when one can, dear old thing," Victor said righteously and winked.

"Well..." Violet mused, pushing her plate aside for her wine glass, "if it's for God's work.

It's decided then. Victor is no longer allowed to gamble with anyone except missionaries, John

Davies will come to our dinner and adore our Gwennie, Lila will return to the lonely arms of Denny, who has, no doubt, consoled himself with moving pictures, chocolates, and fountains of wine. I shall abstain from hunting up my little sister and trying to persuade her to embrace the rights of women and turn away from the same old downtrodden path."

"Alrighty then." Lila tapped a finger to her lips and took a drag of her cigarette. "Enough of degrading married women. As a married woman, I object. Also, I won the race to the altar.

You see before you a pair of rusted, tarnished shackles."

"You don't count, love," Gwennie said, pushing her own plate aside and glancing around the restaurant. It wasn't very full, but the food was good and the fires were lively.

"Denny is your chattel," Victor told Lila. "Not the other way around." His eyes glinted in the low light, and his smirk seemed almost devilish with the way the light cast his elfin face in shadow.

Lila scowled before she laughed. "We are each other's chattel. Take it from this wise old married woman, true love is being the other's chattel. Or something like that. Something more poetic and clever. I can't be sure of cleverness after two Gin Rickeys, wine, and a day of travel.

Violet, darling, if you aren't going to marry, you must get a pug."

"Oh, no." Vi shook her head frantically.

"Or perhaps one of those tiny smooshed-faced spaniels." Lila swirled the contents of her glass, staring at it rather dazedly. After the baths and food, exhaustion was hitting all of them like a load of bricks.

Violet shook her head again, tucking a lock of hair behind her ear and adjusting her pearls. "A dog requires walks."

"A job for beloved Beatrice," Lila stated. "Or Victor's man. Beatrice looks like a girl who'd love to take a dog for a walk as part of her work. She'd probably squeal, clap her hands, and ask if it was really so."

"Dogs need love," Violet countered.

"Which you have in abundance," Victor said. "I am liking this plan. I suppose, on occasion, I could drop a few nuggets of affection towards the furry little blighter. We'll have a garden now, darling. It requires a dog."

Violet shot her brother a quelling look, but he was undeterred.

"This is, I think, a matter for serious thought." He leaned back, crossed his legs, and lit another cigarette.

"If you want a dog, darling, get one." Violet took a long sip of her wine. "What I would like is several fluffy pillows and thick blankets. I know it is wretchedly early, and we are supposed to be bright young things, but I am going to give in to my inner old maid and snuggle down with a book, a pillow, and a cup of cocoa."

"That does sound divine," Gwennie said with a wide yawn, followed by murmured apologies.

"Just imagine how cozy it would be to snuggle up with a pup at your back." Victor took another drag off of his cigarette.

Violet once again tried to shoot her brother a quelling look, but he pretended not to notice.

CHAPTER TWO

Their servants, Giles and Beatrice, had left for the train station rather early with the baggage to get it all sorted out before the rest of party left the hotel. As the train wasn't leaving until 10:00 a.m., Gwennie and Lila were avoiding breakfast for lingering in bed. On Gwennie's part, it was probably because she needed to prepare for her journey, so it was only the twins who were partaking of breakfast.

Violet had a dark gray dress on, her cloche at the ready, with her coat and a small bag with a novel, a notebook, and a pen to see her through the train ride. Her brother only needed a fresh case of cigarettes and a lighter to be happy.

"It'll be rather odd, shan't it? To go back to a nice house rather than the shabby little rooms we had before?" he asked as he lit a cigarette. "I think I shall miss the simplicity of those old rooms."

"Do you think that Aunt Agatha is smiling down on us?" Violet had shaken much of her melancholy from losing Aunt Agatha, but it returned in waves. Familiarity with the pain had made it more bearable.

Losing her aunt was worse, really, than losing her mother. Vi remembered her mother only in wisps of memory. The smell of her perfume, the way the light had glinted through Mama's hair when she leaned down to kiss Vi's head or to scold her with a gentleness that countered any words intended to mold her daughter.

Aunt Agatha had taken up the space where Mama had resided, evolving from the nice aunt who'd spoiled the twins with toys and treats to the woman who had been Violet's guiding light. It was because Aunt Agatha was a revolutionary that Violet was so independent a young woman. Aunt Agatha had never allowed Violet to believe that women were lesser in any way.

What would she have been like, Violet thought, if she'd had only Lady Eleanor? The twins' stepmother was appallingly Victorian. Would Vi have married as young as Isolde was going to? Would Vi have believed that the only purpose to a woman's life was to make a good match and bear children? Violet wasn't against either of those things, and neither had Aunt

Agatha been. But that was not all there was to Violet, nor was it all that there had been to Agatha. She supposed that what Aunt Agatha had done for Violet was not to shift her view of the traditional life but to widen her possibilities.

It was possible to love and be your own person. It was possible to marry and have a life beyond that marriage. It was possible to be both feminine and brilliant at business. The list was as endless as the possibilities of a woman who was determined to reach for her goals.

"I need a new journal, brother dear," Violet said. "I have avoided recording my thoughts since losing Aunt Agatha. I think the time has arrived to discover them once again."

"There is a magic in it, isn't there? I haven't either. Perhaps I shall join you."

"And will you discover the aching need for a wife and children?"

In a moment of rare seriousness, Victor admitted, "I am not against that, darling one. I just want what Aunt Agatha had. We *are* young. Contrary to traditional belief, there is no need to speed ahead."

The moments of seriousness had occurred more and more since Christmas. Aunt Agatha had been murdered over the holidays. Victor and Violet had both ended up as murder suspects and heirs. They eventually found that their beloved aunt had been killed for the inheritance she provided. She'd given her favorite nieces and nephews sufficient income to change their lives, and their cousin Meredith had been unable to wait until God took Aunt Agatha home. Instead, Merry had taken matters into her own hands.

The loss of the woman who had filled the role of their mother coupled with the change in their circumstances had required the twins to spend many an hour discussing everything from their mourning, to business, to how to handle the adjustment of society's view of them. Neither of them were quite sure what to expect of how their own family would react.

Only Father they felt certain of. He'd recommend Violet to find a respectable young man, but make a passing comment about frivolous young women and how he didn't expect she'd follow his advice. Father would offer Victor a cigar and harrumph about not being stupid with his money. Then the earl would go back to late evenings, long smokes, and mild moaning about the state of his horses, fox hunting, and shooting.

Violet and Victor had gone from being able to live a life of leisure with careful spending to...so much more. Victor would be able to indulge in his delight of old books, cigars, and crafting new cocktails with greater ease than ever before.

Violet, on the other hand, had become one of those ridiculously affluent types. Nearly anything was possible with what Aunt Agatha had handed to her niece.

She wore it well, with a smirk and an ease of generosity that hadn't changed. If one had known her before, her manner was quite the same. The only major change was the acquisition of a maid of her own and an utter refusal to ever darn another pair of stockings. Well, that and the inordinate amount of money she'd spent in Paris fashion salons.

Violet had left England with two small trunks. Those had been gifted to the maid and new, significantly larger trunks acquired and stuffed. Vi had even debated a third trunk until Victor had allowed her space in his own. Unlike Violet, who'd kept her old wardrobe, he'd abandoned his and purchased all new. Victor would have teased Vi mercilessly for the excessive clothing shopping if not for the inordinate amount of wine and spirits he'd bought, the boxes upon boxes of cigars. They'd found themselves realizing for the first time they were rich when they'd fallen in love with art and been able to acquire it.

The call to return hadn't been so immediate that they'd needed to hurry home, so they'd enjoyed the journey and the purchases along the way.

———

Later that morning on the train, Gwennie and Lila went straight for a corner seat while

Violet hesitated.

"I..."

"Oh." Gwennie frowned towards Violet and Victor. "Go. I don't want you to see me sick up any more than you want to."

"You're a doll, love." Violet and Victor escaped before guilt had them taking a seat with Lila and Gwennie. Vi wound her arm through Victor's elbow and said, "I want to start writing books again."

He grinned at her. "I thought we were going to live lazily in the life of luxury, doing nothing but dancing and seeing shows, with you acquiring new shoes and me finding just the right shirt for my striped trousers."

She winked before she honestly admitted, "Perhaps, after a few months of idleness, I've realized why Aunt Agatha spent so much time building an empire. Idleness makes me itchy."

"Idleness," he mused. "And messiness, poorly-made clothes, seams in your gloves, the sound of anything that squeaks. I, on the other hand, feel I was made to be idle. It suits me admirably, sister dear, but perhaps if you insist..."

She chuckled and tugged on his arm, making him lean down so she could mockingly whisper, "If you need to blame me for your American puritanicalness, I'll accept the blame for you, darling."

He laughed, but choked in surprise. "Well I'll be demmed. If it isn't Jack Wakefield. How are you, sir?"

Violet started and followed her brother's gaze. The shadow of how and why they'd met Jack colored their thoughts but not their expressions. Jack Wakefield was the man Aunt Agatha had called upon when she realized someone was trying to kill her. If only Aunt Agatha had followed either Vi's or Jack's advice of leaving them to figure things out, Aunt Agatha might have survived.

They'd been unable to save her, but Jack had found the killer in the end. With a little help from Violet's unwarranted interference. Meddling hadn't caused the awareness between Violet and Jack to fade and neither, it seemed, had distance and time.

He was a massive man, with rugged lines and a thick shock of hair. Despite not being quite the current fashion for good looks, he did something to Violet that yanked her attention to him and him alone.

Jack Wakefield was sitting near a window next to a rotund man with a bald head, sharp eyes, and a suit that had seen better days. He looked up at the sound of his name.

"Ah, if it isn't the Carlyle twins. May I make you known to my good friend and former commander, Mr. Hamilton Barnes?"

Violet smiled charmingly at him while Victor's lazy grin proclaimed him far more the spaniel than the lion he kept hidden. As was typical for Victor, his veneer lifted the second they were around anyone else.

Jack noted the switch, and Violet suspected Mr. Barnes saw it as well. She supposed that a man who'd commanded Jack in the military police during the Great War and retained both Jack's friendship and respect would be more clever than a little fat and a worn suit would indicate.

Of course, Victor's tendency towards self-mockery and modern clothes did the same for him—disguised his intensity and brilliance. Violet, on the other hand, disguised herself with merry grins and meaningless chatter whenever it suited her. They were, all of them, actors on life's stage.

Jack's grin was nearly as careless as Victor's when he said, "You've come back to the shores of home? Whatever happened to your plans to indulge in the sun ceaselessly and then think upon America?" Jack's gaze flicked over Violet with the weight of a touch, and she had to fight off a shiver.

"We've been summoned," Victor declared. "Drawn from our natural habitat in the sun and warmth to the home fires. We will, no doubt, be assessed and found wanting."

"Oh that can't be right," Mr. Barnes said, as he glanced between the two of them and then indicated the seats across from him and Jack with a silent invitation.

The twins took up residence across from the men and smiled winningly.

"Clearly," Violet said laughing. "It is utterly incorrect for myself. Angel child, that's me. Victor, however, is a lay-about without good intentions and with a predilection for gambling with missionaries."

"Sister!" Victor clutched his chest. "You wound and disparage me. I was but doing my poor best to assist the good efforts of our Godly minded brethren, and now I find how one is treated after contributing to the needy. Violet shall throw me to the wolves to save herself."

"Every time," Violet said, with a cheeky grin at all three men. She adjusted the cuff of her coat before standing and letting Victor help her out of it.

Jack had stood with them, and his bulk, yet again, sent a shiver of awareness through her.

"Have you all been in Dover?" she asked as a distraction. "Not that exciting of a place with the buckets of spring rain falling."

"Working, I'm afraid," Mr. Barnes said. "Jack here was good enough to shake off the dust of semi-retirement for me on this last case."

Violet glanced at Jack, a question in her gaze, and he said, "Barnes always was the one to drag me into cases. From the war to the present, making a puppet of me. Don't be confused by his hound dog manner. He's a master manipulator."

"Only of you," Mr. Barnes replied. "Jack told me of your recent case. My condolences on your aunt."

Violet nodded, blinking rapidly. "Thank you."

Jack's gaze moved over her face, warming her. She wished she knew what was behind the shutters of his eyes, what he was thinking of her. Did he dislike how she'd interfered? She'd known he was worried that she had, but the danger was over before he knew of the risk. Would he have raked her over the coals if it had been his place? She'd seen the tight expression on his face, but she'd also noted how he'd verified their travel plans. She'd felt at the time he'd cared that she was leaving and it mattered to him when she'd be back. Was that so?

All she could be sure of was that it wasn't disapproval in his gaze at that moment. Not that it necessarily meant anything. He might have a woman back at home he was returning to.

While she'd ensured he wasn't married after they'd met, that didn't mean he wasn't attached.

Violet played with the ring on her finger while they chatted, trying to hide her thoughts.

The glint in her brother's eyes, however, said she was unsuccessful as far as he was concerned.

Mr. Barnes adjusted the conversation to the weather and from the weather to the new silent pictures. After a few minutes, Jack's friend turned the conversation again, inquiring about Violet's likes and dislikes. It wasn't until they'd stopped at the next station and decided to stretch before the train left again that she realized she'd been artfully grilled.

Her brother made no mention of it but his lips twitched here and there. The warmth in Mr. Barnes's gaze as the day progressed told her that he approved of her. If she weren't being such a love-struck ninny, she'd have realized *why* he was grilling her. It didn't occur to her until Victor faded into the London rain after making an excuse about gathering the others, and she was faced with Jack alone.

"I didn't think we'd run into each other again," Jack said, shoving his gloves into his pocket.

"And yet"—she smiled merrily despite her racing heart—"we met on a random train my first full day back into the country."

"Do you believe in fate?" His gaze was more intense than she'd been prepared for.

"Perhaps." Violet adjusted her coat casually, as though she weren't terribly nervous without cause. She was aware of him and herself as she'd never been aware before. His proximity, the exact color of his eyes, the shape of his jaw and the depth of his gaze were almost overwhelming her, and whatever veneer she'd put on was melting under the force of his attention.

"Perhaps?" The question was a light mockery more of himself than her. "Perhaps then you'd be willing to join me for dinner?"

She knew at that moment that her stepmother would never approve. As rich as she now was *and* the daughter of an earl? Never. It wasn't that Jack Wakefield wasn't in the class of the idle rich, but Violet was the daughter of an earl. Perhaps an impoverished daughter of an earl could sink a class beneath her, but a rich one, never. Violet also realized just how much power love could have over her.

She wasn't in love. Yet she knew that she was on the tip of a slippery slope entirely because when Jack looked at her—he saw *her.* The loving niece, the attentive sister. The woman who had insisted on being educated and who worked hard in school. The business person who could handle her aunt's investments but wasn't in love with money. He saw the frivolous side of Vi with her love of clothes and novels. The serious side of her, which was generous and kind. She felt as though she'd been stripped bare for the first time in her life, and despite her utter lack of defenses, she wasn't just found approved, she was found admirable.

But he'd asked a question and she'd yet to answer. Dinner. Yes. She nodded, her thoughts making her blush brilliantly. He couldn't possibly know why, but he gently pressed her hand and they set the date for the very next evening. The arrangements were made as Victor lingered with the porter. Violet had no illusions about what her brother was doing, and it wasn't until Jack took a step back before Victor found he was finished with the porter.

He returned to them at the opportune moment and said, "Hargreaves has sent an automobile for us, darling. Giles and the porter have arranged the baggage. Steady Beatrice has gotten Gwennie and Lila to the vehicle and they wait only for us."

"It was lovely to see you again," Violet told Jack, and Victor echoed her and offered a ride.

"Barnes has abandoned me," Jack admitted. "Work doesn't cease for the virtuous.

Though I can't claim the same attributes, and I thank you for the offer, I am required elsewhere."

They said their goodbyes and the twins joined their friends in the automobile. They dropped Lila and Gwennie at Lila's home before the twins made their way to their new home.

It would be the first time they entered the townhouse as denizens rather than visitors. The realization of where they were going and why changed the moment from excitement to grief.

"It makes her loss seem even more real." Violet's gaze was fixed out the automobile window to hide the tears threatening to fall.

"I'd almost rather go to our old rooms," Victor said.

She could hear the same emotions in his voice, though she gave him the privacy of not looking at him.

"We should have thought it through when we sent Hargreaves to prepare the house and move our things. Our old rooms weren't so bad."

Now that they were free of them rather than making the

best of them, she could admit they had been a step above awful.

"Cheap," Violet sniffed.

"Shabby," Victor admitted.

"Smelling faintly of mildew when it rained."

They both focused on the rain through the glass of their automobile, remembering how their old rooms would smell on a day like today. Violet admitted, "The house was a gift from

Aunt Agatha to you. I'm going to imagine her smiling down on our cherubic heads."

"Cherubic?" Victor snorted. "Not for either of us, darling."

"Cherubic heads," Violet repeated. "I'll just be glad that our home won't smell of mildew, glad to know we're snuggled up in beds that she purchased. She loved us. This is how it should be."

"She did love us," Victor said, swallowing thickly.

"Her love is why..." Violet lost the battle to her tears and took the handkerchief that

Victor had at the ready.

"Her love made us who we are. Without her..."

Violet nodded, blinking a tear away, and then the townhouse was before them. Her brother handed her out of the Silver Ghost. The townhouse didn't proclaim buckets of riches in the manner that Agatha had possessed. It was a grey brick house in a good neighborhood, rather nearer the portions of London that Violet and Victor frequented.

"You know," Victor said, frowning at the house, "she sold that other house a few years ago."

"When we told her...".

They stared at the house. It was the exact type of place they'd have chosen should they have had the money. Nice, solid, not ostentatious.

"This is what you'd have bought," Violet said, no longer

able to hold back her tears. "She sold her old house and bought this one for you. Look at it...it was made for you. It's secure and will protect those you care about. But it isn't so over-the-top that you'd be uncomfortable. And close to the little Chinese food restaurant you love. "

Victor nodded, his jaw was clenching over and over again and finally he ground out,

"How well she knew us."

"How much she loved you."

"Us both." He glanced at Violet and then grinned, losing the melancholy. "She knew you'd eventually give in to the old school fairytale. Love. Children. Home. Is Mr. Jack Wakefield, sometime detective inspector of Scotland Yard, the one who will drag you to the altar?"

"Kicking and screaming," Violet told her brother, but a part of her was very much afraid she was obfuscating.

CHAPTER THREE

Violet's bedroom had always been intended for her. It was as clear as the sun in the sky once she realized the house had been a gift for Victor. The walls were papered with light gray with deeper gray stripes. The furniture was black and heavily masculine, but the touches of feminine accent throughout the room were just what Violet would have chosen.

There was even a desk that was perfect for a typewriter. Violet had to send Beatrice away so that she could explore the bedroom's charms and let her emotions free. She ended up sitting on the edge of her bed, handkerchief in her hand, remembering moment after moment with Aunt

Agatha, Victor, and even Algernon and Meredith. Obviously, much of those memories with Merry, especially, were bittersweet. But hate Meredith's crime as much as Violet did, their childhood had been shared.

Vi and Victor had played with the little metal soldiers in the garden, gone fishing, jumped into the swimming hole, and been read to by Aunt Agatha. How many times had they enjoyed a nursery tea together with Aunt Agatha explaining life and answering their questions? She'd always treated them as capable of learning. She'd been interested in their thoughts, unlike Father and Lady Eleanor, who had preferred the children to be silent.

After Vi was through sniffling over the bedroom, she noted the two armoires certainly intended for her love of clothing. There was a red and gray Chesterfield near the window and a pair of matching armchairs near the fire. The nice chest at the end of the bed was likely intended to give Violet a place to tuck things away. Aunt Agatha had never been bothered by Vi's need for things to be orderly and put away. The final gift was a large, three-paneled mirror.

When she finally had herself under control, she had Beatrice and a tea tray up to her room. The maid dealt with Vi's clothes, chattering about the traveling they'd done since Beatrice came to work for Violet. While Beatrice carried on her monologue, Violet arranged her pulp novels and magazines in the chest at the end of her bed. She'd need to buy herself a bookshelf for her room eventually, but for now, they could be arranged by title and author in her trunk or by publication name for the magazines.

She laughed at herself as she arranged things just so, but there was something about having one's books unpacked and available that proclaimed one was home.

"Beatrice," Violet said, "tomorrow have Mr. Giles come up here to review the furniture and then request him to find me a few bookshelves for my bedroom. I won't be truly at home until I have them. In fact...yes...have him find bookshelves with cabinet doors."

"Yes, miss. Mr. Giles does have such good taste. I've heard Lord Victor say so."

"Better than both Victor and me, I'm afraid," Violet laughed. "Are you ready to work in the city now? Do you wish to return home? I'm sure Mr. Davies would hire you for your old post."

"Oh no, miss." Beatrice shook her head a little frantically. "I love working for you, caring for your pretty things and..."

Violet realized that she'd unintentionally upset Beatrice and went about comforting her before she returned to arranging her bedroom. If she were someone else, she might have thrown herself on her bed and rested. She wouldn't be truly comfortable, however, until her things were arranged.

It was only when she set up her desk that she realized she could have a typewriter of her own now. No longer would she and Victor have to share for their stories. She kept forgetting that she didn't have to watch her purchases so carefully anymore.

Victor knocked on her open door. "Oh, well this room was made for you, wasn't it?"

Violet told Victor of her plans for using his man to get new shelving and he said, "Darling, there's a little room down the hall that can be your office and pulp novel hideaway. It's empty. You'll need to outfit it with whatever your heart desires."

Her gaze narrowed on him. "It's the office for the lady of the house, isn't it?"

He smirked and attempted to look innocent.

"And because I am a lady, I am suddenly in charge of maids and meals?"

He begged without saying a word.

"Very well," she said. "But I am giving it up the moment you succumb to the finer emotions."

"Darling, you're already succumbing to those emotions. Did you think I was unaware of the glances between you and a certain Mr. Wakefield? Sharpen your skills upon my household while you fight your fate, and your hulking investigator will thank me for it."

She scowled at him. "Were you here just to put me to work or was there something else?"

He frowned and pulled an envelope from his pocket. "Sneaking home did us no good, darling. They've found us."

Violet turned her scowl towards the envelope. It was the same thick cream paper and red seal that Lady Eleanor always used. Vi had been certain they'd have a few days to settle in, and yet here was a summons.

"What madness is this? We have only just arrived. Did you call ahead? How did they know?"

He shook his head. "Perhaps Lady Eleanor has employed a spy."

"Find the fiend out and send them on their way," Violet demanded, her gaze still fixed on the hated envelope. Then she sighed and admitted, "She always does outwit us when she chooses. Our problem is that we never expect her attack until it's too late. Well...out with it.

What is the sentence?"

"A dinner party. Thursday. With Isolde, the betrothed, our esteemed stepmother, and a few select guests."

"I suppose it was inevitable, wasn't it?"

"At least we'll have the shield of a good cocktail."

"Of course, dear one." Violet smirked at him. She preferred to drink when she was happy, not to dull her senses in dealing with family, so she'd be lingering over one drink rather than drowning herself in her cups.

He scowled at her and warned, "Two can play at that game."

"Will you be sneaking a flask into tea with Lady Eleanor? Didn't she cut you off the last time?"

He laughed. "Picture her face."

"Oh I am," Violet countered, raising a thin brow. "Finding you guzzling from a flask during her dinner party will have Father on our doorstep."

"Perhaps the flask only in the automobile."

"Wiser, but I think you'd better save it for after, darling. You'll need all of your defenses."

Violet set Beatrice to freshen the dress for the dinner party and another for her date, and then took the typewriter from Victor and dropped herself into a story. She was flying through a tale of a haunted house, a young ingénue, and her lover with a dark past. The hours passed until Victor came to her room.

"Dear one, give me your pages and go to bed. You'll need your wits tomorrow to enchant

Jack and then to deal with Lady Eleanor."

Violet shook herself from the specter scene she'd been writing. "Is it so late?" She stretched and yawned and realized it was deep into the night. "It's like visiting an old friend. I forget how much writing makes you visit different parts of your head. I feel as though there were cobwebs up there after all of our time being good-for-nothings."

"Parts of your head?" He laughed at her and gathered up the stack of pages. "Bed, dear one."

"Perhaps it has been too long," Violet said, gesturing to the pages, "and it's all a jumble of words and nonsense. Pulp stories have nothing redeemable about them but fun, and I'm not sure I delivered even that much."

"Certainly nothing but fun," he agreed.

"What do you think Lady Eleanor would say if she knew how we'd kept ourselves in eggs and sardines before the influx of the ready money?" Their secret writing career and the pseudonym for the duo of V.V. Twinnings was a secret that only their closest friends knew. "She'd turn over in her grave and scream down the house, darling. Our secret must never get out."

Violet laughed as she turned in her chair and then glanced down at herself. She still wore her traveling clothes and hadn't done much more than slide off her shoes. She picked them up and put them away while Victor said, "Shall I call for a warm milk?"

"I'll have a bath and be fine. No need to wake Beatrice or Hargreaves to coddle me."

Victor nodded as she grabbed one of her books, winking at him, and left him stealing the pages of what she'd written while she made her way to her private bath. She hadn't noted the taps on the bath before, but the Asian style dragon that poured water from its mouth made her smile. Yet again, Aunt Agatha reflecting her love for Violet through the little details.

If there was anything that being independent did, it was to give you the freedom to indulge harmless vices without reproach. She started her bath with rose-scented pink salts and then sank into the hot water and the newest Tarzan novel without another thought.

The next morning, Violet donned a new dress she'd purchased in Paris. It was a very light pink, almost nude in color, with lace edging and simple lines. She had a matching cloche hat and a drawstring bag. She finished dressing with a pair of small pearl ear bobs, a long strand of pearls, and some barely there color on her lips.

"Am I presentable?" she asked her brother as she went down the stairs.

He nodded and they went to the business offices.

"Lord Carlyle," the clerk said as they walked in, and then a moment later, "Lady Carlyle."

They hadn't made an appointment, but considering that Violet owned these offices, she smiled brightly and said, "Lovely day, isn't it? We'll be seeing Fredericks."

The clerk sort of started. "Well yes, of course, my lady. Did you want tea?"

Violet shook her head and glanced at Victor, making a passing comment on the office furniture.

"Did my lady wish to wait out here?"

Victor cleared his throat, mouth twitching as Violet turned and asked, "Why would I want to do that?"

"Ah..."

Violet's tone had been bright and charming, but the clerk seemed to sense the trap as the door behind him opened.

"Well...I just hoped to avoid your boredom?"

"Because my pretty little head cannot possibly understand business."

"Well...ah...."

Hamilton Fredericks scowled at his clerk. "Jones, you fool. Lady Carlyle, Lord Carlyle, please this way."

After a conversation about the state of the business and Violet signing a few papers, Vi leaned back and said, "Thank you for being good at what you do."

"Thank you for actually reading the reports I send you. I know that others aren't so lucky as I. Too often business deals are made among folks over dinner or a polo match, ignoring the advice of fellows such as myself."

Violet glanced at Victor who knew it was as true as she did. "Well...I promise not to disemploy you, should the day arrive you feel the need to call me to account."

Fredericks grinned for a moment. "I have little doubt that I will never need to, my lady.

I..." He glanced a little anxiously between the twins. "I hesitate to--"

"Out with it, man," Victor said as he sipped the coffee he'd accepted from the clerk.

"It's not my place. I know that."

"You're forgiven in advance, Mr. Fredericks. Please tell us what is on your mind."

Mr. Fredericks pushed back his glasses and pulled out a register. "Your sister, Lady Isolde?"

"Yes," Violet said, feeling a hint of trepidation.

"Her betrothed came here and wished me to place some money into his investment scheme. He alluded, rather forcefully, that you were behind this plan."

Violet paused, a flash of rage rushing through her though nothing reflected on her face.

Her brother reached out and touched her wrist. A lodestone to help keep her anger in check.

"And?"

"My lady, Italy is not so far and I had not heard from you. I know you give me rather a lot of latitude to follow my instincts in business. Ultimately, I told a little...well...a...a fabrication..."

Victor grinned and snorted back a laugh, "So you told Danvers what? That Violet does not allow you to fly free?"

"Just so," Mr. Fredericks said, "that I wasn't able to make any such investment until I heard from you directly. But I did look into the scheme, ma'am. I thought if I were mistaken on his intentions I should be prepared with the advice I normally provide."

Violet crossed her fingers in her lap and waited. She liked nothing about the situation and even with encouragement to invest, she didn't think she'd follow it. She had solid investments with people who didn't try to manipulate and lie their way into accessing her money.

"I'm alarmed," Mr. Fredericks admitted. "The amounts I hear bandied about for Mr.

Danvers's wealth don't match up with what I've learned as I researched."

Victor was the one who leaned forward at that point. He lost his lazy spaniel look and asked silkily, "So Danvers is not as rich as he reports himself to be?"

Fredericks shook his head. "I believe it is a...house of cards."

"And those who've invested with him?" Victor's face was impassive stone and Violet shivered.

"Are in a rather precarious fiscal situation."

Violet licked her lips, playing with the ring on her finger while she closed her eyes. It was worse than Fredericks could possibly know. Would her sister be marrying this Danvers if he were not rich? Of course she wouldn't, though perhaps Danvers wouldn't be marrying Isolde if not for her wealthy connections. Violet doubted it very much. The way he'd attempted to manipulate Fredericks told her Danvers was a man without honor. But also without money?

She scowled. Danvers was using this new connection to Isolde to get access to Violet's funds. She was suddenly certain that to Mr. Danvers, the prize was not Isolde, but her rich connections.

CHAPTER FOUR

Jack Wakefield in his evening clothes was enough to steal Violet's breath and keep it captive. She smiled through it, walked down to his automobile with her hand on his arm. His bulk made her feel delicate, though she was hardly that, and the glint in his eyes made her feel beautiful. She hadn't expected a pretty little Austin 7 when she'd imagined his car, but it seemed to suit him when he opened the door for her.

"I confess," he said as he handed her inside of the vehicle, "I was a little uncertain of where to bring you. I suppose you like jazz and dancing and clubs?"

Violet nodded and admitted, "All of the usual things."

"Would you like to try something rather adventurous?" There was a certain tilt to his lips that was full of good humor, and his eyes were alight with challenge.

"Of course," she said merrily, laughing up at him. Her heart was in her throat, her veins were racing with anticipation, and she felt suddenly certain that she had always been intended to be right in this car, at right this moment, with this man. He had a seriousness to him that didn't try to crush her light-heartedness. "You see before you a woman who fears nothing...let alone whatever it is you have planned."

His laugh was deep, and she felt warmed by it. She hadn't heard it from him much.

Things had been too dark and too serious when they'd been trying to stop Aunt Agatha's murder. He didn't explain his plan, simply wove his little automobile through the streets of London, parked, and handed her out onto a rather hole-in-the-wall-place. Most of the people nearby were of Indian descent.

Jack grinned at her and asked, "Do you like spicy food?"

"I'd have said yes, but I believe that most of the Indian food I've had was adjusted for our weaker palates."

"Next time, we'll go to the Criterion." Jack ordered for both of them and the food was quite different from what she was used to. Red sauce, rice, and interesting white chunks in it. She took her first bite tentatively and nodded at his somewhat anxious gaze. It wasn't spicy at all, though he had ordered several spicy things. She waved her hand in front of her face when her nose started burning and had to carefully dab away the tears from her eyes to protect the kohl on her eyes.

They were getting sideways looks from the other restaurant goers, but once she laughed off the burning, the other patrons went back to their food.

"This isn't hot," she said, pointing to the red sauce with white chunks. "What are these things?"

"They're called paneer. I lived in India for a while and have been unable to return to our blander foods here. Though, you can't beat our fish and chips."

"A favorite," she admitted. "I missed them quite a bit when we were in Italy. Though already I'm regretting not having easy access to veal marsala."

It was easy to move from favorite foods to favorite books

to favorite pastimes. Despite the changing clientele, who came in work clothes and grabbed dinner, Violet and Jack lingered over their food.

She didn't even notice time passing until Jack said, "I don't believe this evening will be a success until we dance."

That was an offer she would never turn down. The night-club, like the restaurant, was a bit of a hole-in-the-wall, though she barely noticed the dark walls, the clouds of smoke, or the crowded room. He swung her into a dance that left her breathless and laughing. A moment later, her gaze was caught by a couple in the corner.

At first, she was just appalled that they were kissing so openly. The man had slick-backed hair and a triple set of chins. The young woman before him had to be younger than even Violet, and she had to be half his age.

"Oh," she said, blinking rapidly as though the smoke had somehow disguised what she was seeing. It hadn't.

"Are you all right?" Jack asked into her ear, having to lean down to reach her.

She started to say yes and then shook her head.

"Perhaps a drink?" she suggested, and Jack wove them off the dance floor, people moving out of his way instinctively.

"What would you like to drink?"

She shrugged and the bartender grinned at her, eyes up. Violet turned to him and asked,

"What do you recommend?"

"Always the house drink," he said, in a way that made it clear he didn't recommend it at all.

Violet winked at the man. He was spiffy in a nice suit, with dark skin, hair, and eyes. His expression twinkled as Violet asked, "What if I resolutely turn the house drink down?"

"Would you like something new?"

Violet nodded, glancing up at Jack, who said, "I think we both would."

The man mixed them two drinks and handed them over. "This is called The Sidecar."

Violet took a careful sip. "Mmm."

"What is that?" Jack asked.

"Cognac, orange liqueur, and lemon juice. Do you like it?"

"Very much," Violet agreed. She begged the ratios from him for Victor before grinning up at Jack.

"How long may I keep you?" The question was light, but Violet felt as though if she answered forever, he'd take her up on the dare.

"Not too late, I'm afraid," she said, but she placed her hand on his wrist so he'd know she wasn't escaping him. "My stepmother is having a dinner party tomorrow, and I have to show up with bells and smiles on to meet the scoundrel-in-law."

He laughed. "Already you've decided to dislike him?"

"Early reports are...alarming."

A look of concern appeared as he led her towards the hall. They went right past that large man, who noticed her attention. He narrowed his gaze upon her, flicking over her meanly before turning back to his companion, as though Violet were the one who was acting amiss.

Jack drove her home, walking her to the door. He pressed a solitary finger under her chin to turn her face up to his. The move made her wish for a kiss and her heart raced at that simple touch. The porch light put them in a circle of radiance while all around them was dark and silent.

It wasn't the early hours of the morning, but it was nearer than not.

"Thank you for your company," he said with a gentle smile.

Violet grinned and curtsied in reply.

"May I call upon you again?"

"Oh, I'd say so." Vi winked as he squeezed her hand before seeing her inside of Victor's house.

————

"I thought I wouldn't see you until the early hours." Victor stepped out from the library as Violet shut the front door.

"I thought you were going out," she told him. "What's this? Shirtsleeves, a tie hanging around your neck, and ruffled hair?"

"I was going to meet Denny and Lila, only then I had an idea for the story. I just had to get it down. The next thing I knew, you were coming through the door. Didn't it go well?"

"Oh, Jack was...well." Violet cleared her throat, knowing she was blushing, and her brother laughed back at her.

After meeting Jack, she was suddenly willing to consider a different future—if he was who she thought. He had charms enough to bend her will towards that path. She slowly undressed, putting away her jewelry, hanging up her dress, arranging her shoes and her coat where they belonged before noticing an amethyst book on her desk. There was a lovely pen next to it.

Victor must have made a stop at some point or sent out Giles. The journal was just what she wanted. Vi put on a kimono that Victor had purchased for her in Italy and then a robe. Slipping her feet into warm slippers, she sat down at her desk. Her mind was moving too quickly towards including Jack in all things, and it was worrying her.

Was she intrigued by him and attracted? Yes. Had they bonded over a quite intense period over the holidays? Yes. But could she trust her future to the instincts that came out of those weeks? No. Who was Jack when the pressure wasn't on? Who was he when his father wasn't in the house and he hadn't been brought in to be the savior?

And, for that matter, he wasn't even offering anything other than another dinner and perhaps another dance.

Vi quite wanted to shake herself. Perhaps it was Isolde's fate of marrying so quickly that had Violet's mind skipping ahead without using rational, logical steps.

Violet sketched out her thoughts in her journal and came to the conclusion that as much as she liked Jack—and oh, she did—she could not possibly race ahead. Not when her future was so wrapped up in such a decision.

CHAPTER FIVE

The evening of the dinner party, Violet twirled in front of her brother in one of her new Parisian evening gowns. It was a dark teal green with a gold lace overlay. With wide straps and a rather higher neckline, it was near modesty while still having the Eastern opulence that Violet loved.

She wore a long strand of pearls and a feather and pearl headpiece with the lightest amounts of kohl and rouge, leaving her the bright young thing she was without attempting to push her stepmother too far.

Victor frowned at her. "Dearest darling, nothing you wear will be sufficient for our garrulous stepmother, especially with Isolde present. I say slather on the rouge, thicken up that black stuff on your eyes, and wear the dress with the pink fringe."

Victor's hair was slicked back and he wore a grey suit with a vest and a blue tie, and he carried a cane with a dragon's head at the tip.

"You look dashing, Victor," she told him, laughing merrily and then pointing out,

"Certainly whomever our dear stepmother has invited for you will find you handsome indeed."

Violet joined him in the back of the Silver Ghost. Giles drove the automobile through the busy streets to the ancient Carlyle house, which was lit up with shadows in the windows.

"Courage, dear one," Victor said, speaking to them both.

They'd considered time and again if Lady Eleanor would become more commanding or less now that they were settled financially, and they'd never been able to reach a conclusion. "It's not like we don't already know she favors her children." Vi adjusted her dress and looked up at the house that had never felt as much like home as Aunt Agatha's.

Before they could knock, the butler, Thornton, opened the door. "Lady Violet." There was a light in his eye that said he remembered when he'd helped them sneak biscuits from the kitchens. "Lord Victor. They are waiting for you in the blue salon."

Victor held out his arm, and Violet put her hand on his elbow and squeezed. Neither of them took much note of the oversized foyer or the staircase that curved up to an opulent landing with large paintings for each step. The painted ceilings and ancient crystal chandeliers overhead didn't garner a blink. This had long since become old hat.

Thornton opened the salon door and Lady Eleanor turned with a bright smile. There was a crowd of gentlemen and ladies present who were more Lady Eleanor's age than Violet would have guessed for a dinner party for her younger half-sister.

She recognized her stepmother's brother and cousin right away, both of whom nodded to the twins. Markus Kennington was the brother of Lady Eleanor while Norman was the cousin.

Violet smiled at both of them without quite allowing them to draw her into their conversations. Victor hummed under his breath, and the veneer of the light-hearted spaniel dropped over him without a flicker of a lash.

"Wonderful." Lady Eleanor presented her cheek for a kiss. "We've missed you both. You're the last to arrive, so we can enjoy drinks."

Violet's answering smile didn't reach her eyes, but Lady Eleanor either didn't notice or didn't care. Of course, Lady Eleanor's face and tone didn't reflect the irritation Violet was sure her stepmother felt. How dare they be the last of the guests to appear?

"Don't you look lovely," Lady Eleanor said to Violet, and then turned to Isolde.

Violet took in the sight of her sister. She still looked alarmingly young. Her long blonde hair was pulled back into an elegant chignon and her dress was a charming light pink with layers of fringe. It formed to her body, as Isolde had more curves than was quite the thing. Violet's slender frame was more in fashion—a lucky happenstance, for she did not watch what she ate.

Standing next to her was a man who made Isolde seem more than young—a mere babe. This fellow was nothing more than a cradle snatcher. He niggled at Violet's mind and then she realized that *this* was the man Violet had seen kissing a woman in the nightclub. A woman who was *not* her sister.

She was quite sure he recognized her as well. Violet fiddled with the ring on her finger and then turned to grin at Thornton as he passed around a tray of drinks, happy for the distraction. She made a surprised face as Thornton showed her the two options.

"Thornton, the man of the hour." She grinned at him. "What are these delights?"

"Lady Isolde wanted unusual drinks this evening, but there is another tray of gin and tonic going about if you'd prefer, m'lady."

Violet tossed him a saucy wink and said, "Oh, I want something exciting and new. How clever of Isolde to have you sleuth out new drinks."

"Well then, m'lady, the slightly yellow drink is called the bee's knees."

"What a fun name. And the pretty reddish one?"

"That is the aviation fizz."

"Frivolous and delightful." Violet took the reddish one and turned back to Victor. "You try the other and we'll switch."

Lady Eleanor's face had frozen with poorly disguised irritation as Violet chose her drink. Vi looked over and saw her father with a scotch in his hand. She winked at him across the room and he started towards them with their eldest brother, Gerald, in tow.

Lady Eleanor turned to Isolde as Violet's smile transformed from blank to forced. "Darling, you should consider a bob like Violet's. It sets off the line of her neck and jaw so well. You both have those lovely fox lines in your features. That comes from the Carlyle line. Though you get your coloring from me and Violet gets hers from her mother. Equally lovely, really. Like different sides of the same coin."

Vi blinked rapidly and glanced at Victor, whose mouth was twitching. They each lifted their drinks and sipped to avoid needing to answer.

"May I present Mr. Danvers," Isolde asked, smiling prettily. "My betrothed."

Victor's spaniel demeanor was in full-force as he choked back the protective elder brother.

"Oh that's sweet," Victor murmured as he lowered his drink. He stepped in with greetings while Violet recovered herself.

Mr. Danvers was 50 years old if he was a day. He was beyond rotund to full fat, and he had a mean twist to his mouth. There were large rings on three of his fingers and his slicked back hair smelled. And, of course, Violet had seen him kissing another woman just the evening before.

Isolde's smile was serene, though she was careful to adjust her hand so Violet could see the large diamond on her finger.

"What a lovely ring," Violet said, pasting a vacuous expression on her face. She took another sip of her drink.

"Darling girl," her father said, placing a hand on her shoulder and squeezing before he shook Victor's hand. "How was the coast?"

Violet chattered about the art while Victor made passing comments about some fellow he'd met who was a friend of their father.

Isolde cut in before long, looking a little aggrieved. Had they been leaving her out? Violet hadn't congratulated her sister but that level of a lie was quite beyond Vi at the moment. Instead, she commented on Isolde's dress.

Vi's acting ability was pressed to its limit and past. Not only had her stepmother not attacked either of the twins with their deficits—a previously favorite pastime—Isolde had been encouraged to be more like Violet. That had never happened in the entirety of Isolde's life.

Violet sidestepped Victor and Danvers before dinner to speak with her father and found him smiling down at her.

"Haven't much liked how you flit about with Victor since you and Vic graduated from college, darling. Now I'd like to see Isolde do a bit of the same. Bit young, isn't she, to be getting wed?"

"Indeed, Father," Violet said, tucking her hand into his elbow and squeezing his arm a little.

He sipped his scotch. "Tried to put a bit of a slow down on it, if I'm being honest. Not sure what to think of this Danvers. Too old and fat for Isolde, but she just chatters to me about clothes. Not like you at all."

Violet nibbled the corner of her mouth before speaking.

"Well, of course, she isn't, Father. We were always quite different."

He simply tutted and took another drink of his scotch. "Girls these days. So busy dancing and drinking and buying shoes that they've forgotten their old fathers."

Violet smiled up at him and said, "Have I forgotten you then, Papa? I remembered you when Victor and I were finding you some Campari, sweet vermouth, and limoncello."

"You think I don't know Victor was hunting those up for himself? As though all I do is drink."

Violet kissed her father's cheek. "We still thought of you when we bought some for you, Papa. What shall we do about Isolde?"

"I don't think there's much left to do, little one." Father sighed and then took another drink from his scotch. A moment later, Thornton announced dinner, and they were separated and led in to dinner with as much ceremony as Lady Eleanor was able to drum up.

Violet was brought into dinner by a fellow named Hugo Danvers. He had to be near their brother Gerald's age, who was a good ten years older than the twins and even older than Isolde. Poor Danvers would be Isolde's future son-in-law and seemed too aware of the ridiculousness of it. Violet's lips twitched at that and she met Victor's gaze, directing his gaze to Hugo with a glance and then back to the others.

Lady Eleanor had included twelve couples. The ones Violet didn't know were two of Mr. Danvers's good friends. Both were married, with spoiled looking wives. They all seemed to be rather too interested in Violet's inheritance.

One of them, a Mr. Jenkins, tried to draw out details over the fish, but Violet sidestepped. His wife tried again over the salad. The friend, Mr. Gulliver, tried during the fruit and cheese. By the time she escaped the table, she felt as pursued as a fox during hunting season.

Violet could hardly believe they even dared to approach her about it. She knew Aunt

Agatha's fortune was gossiped over, but it wasn't the thing to demand those details.

After dinner, she was cornered by them and Danvers. Violet swallowed back her rising irritation and pasted a smile on her face.

Mr. Gulliver asked again, "Now, you inherited when your aunt, Mrs. Agatha Davies, died?"

Violet nodded. "Myself and several cousins."

"But you received the bulk of it?"

Violet frowned. "We were all quite fortunate."

Mr. Danvers cut in with a quelling look at his friend. "Talked to your man of business recently," he told her.

"Did you?" Violet smiled prettily, and her brother coughed into his drink.

"Nincompoop," Danvers snarled. "Mine is a much better choice."

Victor's cough became choked as Violet fluttered her lashes up at Danvers and said, "I'm afraid I have no head for business."

"Women don't," Mr. Danvers said firmly. "I'll take over for you."

"However," she said, smiling, "Mr. Hamilton Fredericks is one of the most respected businessmen in the whole of London, as evidenced both by his wisdom in working for a woman, my aunt, and learning from her."

"Foolishness."

"And of course," Violet cut in brightly, "she took a respectable amount of money and made it something that Midas himself would envy, so perhaps your theory on the capacity of women is ill-formed, old-fashioned, and misogynistic."

Victor choked again and then hastily drained his glass to

cover his laughter.

"Now, my dear," Mr. Danvers slid in. "A mannish woman like your aunt is unique. You can't expect the same successes she had."

"I have no need of those successes. I have quite the fortune without the need to further it with risky, unwise ventures. I will continue to follow the advice of my well-learned and respectable man of business with enough under-standing in my vacant, female head to recognize the best course of action is to separate family and business." Violet smirked up at Victor. "I believe I'll try that bee's knees, brother. You didn't share yours with me at all."

She let go of his arm and stepped away, entirely unsuc-cessful in hiding her fury. She took a drink from Thornton and made her way to the window to glance out. A moment later, she found Danvers had cornered her.

"I saw you with that...Chief Inspector." "I saw you with the harlot," Violet said.

"Don't think I won't tell your mother."

"Don't think I won't tell Isolde."

"Isolde isn't so foolish as yourself and knows the way of the world."

Violet hoped very much that wasn't true.

Danvers took hold of Violet's arm and hissed, "You better watch what you say to me, my dear. You don't want me for an enemy."

"I don't want you for anything," Violet told him. "I find you alarming and disgusting and despise the way you tried to lie and manipulate your way to my finances."

Danvers squeezed tighter on her bicep and the sting was shocking, but Violet didn't let it cross her face.

Without acknowledging his vice grip, she added, "I also found you appalling when I saw your display with that female."

She twisted her arm away, and then she leaned in and said, "I find that I am horrified for my sister. But alarmed for myself? Please."

"Your Father..."

"Does not like you."

"Your brother..."

"Victor?"

Danvers nodded sharply. "He'll listen to a man of the world and step in like needs to be done."

Violet laughed and stepped away.

He said as she left him, "You don't want me for an enemy, foolish girl."

CHAPTER SIX

Violet woke to a slight tapping on her door. "Lady Violet..."
She groaned and rolled onto her side.

"Lady Violet....Lady Eleanor is awaiting you in the parlor."

Violet groaned into her pillow. "Why?"

"I..." Beatrice's stutter had Violet pushing herself up and
shoving off her eye mask.

"Coffee," Violet said. "Aspirin. Victor. Tell my stepmother
to get comfortable."

Beatrice returned while Violet was washing her face and
running a comb through her hair.

She dabbed a little rouge on her cheeks and lips, blinking
blearily at the maid.

"It wasn't a horrible dream? My stepmother really has
arrived?"

"She has, m'lady."

Violet scowled at the girl, noting the tray with an ominous
looking glass that smelled terrible and spicy. She turned to the
girl and asked, "What's this then?"

"Mr. Giles sent it to you, m'lady."

Violet lifted the glass, took the aspirin from the small porcelain dish, and then plugged her nose and swallowed it all. When she was done, she shivered then dropped her robe.

"Hand me a dress," Violet demanded.

"Any dress?"

"Any dress," Violet replied. She grabbed a pair of stockings while Beatrice picked out a dress, shoes, and jewelry. Violet put the things on almost blindly, not really noting what she was wearing until she stood and glanced into the paneled mirror. She found a lacy light pink dress with a tie above the décolletage made out of the same material as the dress.

Violet picked up a piece of toast that had been brought up on the tray, took a long breath in, and then nibbled.

"I suppose I should hurry down," she said, taking a seat and pouring herself a cup of coffee. She added creamer and sugar and then hurried through the toast and coffee. Just before she was finished, Victor knocked on her door.

"Are you ready?"

Violet shot him a look. "The aspirin and whatever that... concoction Giles manifests have not yet started to assist my poor head."

"If we linger too long, we'll—"

"Hear about it long enough that we'll need another aspirin."

Victor pulled Violet unceremoniously to her feet, taking her last piece of toast. "At least you ate, love. I fought fate too long for even coffee. Though I'll have Beatrice bring in tea and biscuits. Maybe if we focus on those, the raking over the coals won't be so bad."

He held out his arm, and they made their way down the stairs. "It seems accurate," Violet told him, "that the maiden voyage of your parlor will be with Lady Eleanor. To be honest, I haven't even stuck my nose in yet."

"Nor have I. We've been busy, love."

Violet sniffed. "I'm ready for a long lie-in and a day without appointments or shopping."

"I'm not sure that our stepmother will let you have that. She'll try to drag you along to whatever she's doing for Isolde to ensure you are aware just what you are missing in refusing to put on a ball and chain."

Violet opened the parlor door and paused when her stepmother turned a furious gaze to her.

"There you are!"

"Were we expecting you?" Violet asked smoothly, crossing to the Chesterfield and taking a seat as Victor joined her.

"I didn't expect you to be layabouts!"

"I don't know why not," Violet said, pressing a finger to her temple and trying to hide a wince. "Unemployed and spoiled added to a late evening with you."

"You drink too much. I won't have you two becoming nothing but drunken layabouts."

Violet sighed in relief as Beatrice entered the parlor with the tea trolley and poured them all a cup. She handed her stepmother her tea with lemon and added far too much milk and sugar to hers, necessities at a time like this.

"I understand," Lady Eleanor said coolly, "that you were quite rude to Mr. Danvers."

Violet sipped her tea slowly, refusing to answer until she thought her reply through. Carefully she set the cup back on the saucer. "I dislike him greatly. However, my behavior was... appropriate considering his."

"This is a very good match for your sister, and I won't have you ruining it."

"I would give my fortune away to ruin it. That man is a cad and a fraud."

Violet took a biscuit and patted Victor on the back, who'd choked at her reply. Lady

Eleanor's gaze narrowed on Violet.

"I did not ask for your opinion. Isolde wasn't so blessed as you just were. Though why? I don't know."

"Agatha wasn't related to Isolde?"

Lady Eleanor's mouth tightened. "You will not ruin this marriage."

"I will endeavor to do my very best for just that end."

"Stepmother, Vi..." Victor said consolingly, "what..."

"Enough out of you, Victor," Lady Eleanor shot out. "You are the reason Vi thinks she can do whatever she wishes. Your support gives her the freedom she'd never otherwise have.

Flitting about like a...a...hussy! And with a Scotland Yard man! How could you, Violet?"

Violet leaned back, crossing her ankles and took another sip of her tea.

"Jack?" Vi finally asked.

"Jack!" Lady Eleanor hissed as though the name were a byword.

"Jack Wake..." Victor started to explain, and Violet placed a hand on her brother.

His explanation cut off, Violet said, "Who I choose to spend my time with will *never* be influenced by you, Lady Eleanor. You have sold Isolde to an old, fat fraud who will leave her miserable, and you know it."

Lady Eleanor placed a hand on her chest and hissed, "Fraud? You have no ground for such a declaration, and money does a lot to bring about happiness, you ungrateful shrew."

Violet slowly put down her teacup and asked, "And if he isn't rich?"

"Of course, he is! My brother and my cousin have invested a large portion of their funds with him and are seeing good returns. Mr. Danvers is a man of financial brilliance."

"Returns? Or promises of good returns? They are very different things, you know."

"What do you know of it? You aren't Agatha Davies. You are a headstrong, arrogant girl who..."

"That is quite enough," Victor said. "Lady Eleanor, Violet has good cause for her concerns about Danvers. I think we can all see, however, your opinion is fixed. I won't have my house sent into chaos so you can expel your differing notions at each other."

Victor rose and handed Lady Eleanor to her feet. "Always lovely to see you, Stepmother.

Hopefully next time we'll all be in better spirits."

He walked her to the door and saw her out as Violet gaped.

The second he returned to the parlor, Vi couldn't hold back her tirade about the terrible match.

"She is so pleased with herself! They...they...they act as though Isolde weren't rich, beautiful, and well-connected. She can't possibly love that Danvers fellow. Where is her spine?

Where are her dreams? What is wrong with her? By Jove, Victor!"

"I know, darling," he said, sounding as sick as Violet.

"We must do something."

"There's nothing to be done, darling. I've been desperate to come up with a plan. There's nothing. If we intrude and infuriate Isolde, we leave her with only her...*mother.*" He said the word as though it were a terrible insult.

"You don't even know the half of it, Vic," Violet moaned. "I...I...saw a man snogging in the club where Jack took me dancing. I was appalled, of course, but I didn't think anything of it. It was Danvers!"

"With Isolde?" Victor asked, horrified. "Necking in a club!"

"No! That's the worst of it. Oh, Victor...it wasn't even her. He isn't being true to her, he's horrible, Fredericks doesn't even think he's as rich as he says...and Lady Eleanor will never believe me."

"It's criminal!" Victor stood suddenly, starting a route around the parlor with his pacing, and Violet found she was following the opposite path. Worry for Isolde rolled over her skin like a thousand ants.

"You know Lady Eleanor as well as I do," Violet moaned. "Her math always adjusts towards her darling son. Marry off Isolde well and she won't need the inheritance. Get us out of the way, and surely Father will leave Geoffrey the money that was once intended for us. I never imagined that would extend to Isolde, but I suppose I was foolish."

Victor grunted, dropped into his seat, and downed his tea.

"What if you said something to Father?" She spun towards her brother, tone desperate even though she knew the answer already. Father had tried to stop this. He hadn't known everything, but would he believe them over Lady Eleanor's family? The elder generation? Violet didn't think he would.

Victor shook his head.

"What about Gerald? He isn't one to be uncaring."

Victor sighed. "Darling, I'll track him down. But I suppose we must accustom ourselves to being connected to Danvers."

"Never," Violet swore, hoping for a miracle. "Never. We must come up with a plan, we must...we must...rally round. We must call on the troops. We must find out if Danvers really does have a house of cards in various investments and is a fraud."

———

They'd called for their friends to arrive at luncheon and brainstorm, and when Violet entered the parlor just before the appointed hour, she'd found that their company had arrived. Lila had already helped herself to mixing up a round of mint juleps, as Violet had intended to do before her friends showed up.

"Hullo! Hullo! How's kicks, sweet things?" The doorbell rang as Violet spoke, and she slowly turned to face the door with a frown on her face. If it was Lady Eleanor again, Vi was going to hide.

A moment later, Hargreaves said, "Mr. Jack Wakefield has arrived, m'lady."

Her brows rose and she glanced behind her. They all knew him anyway, and surely a military man would be capable of helping them design a campaign?

"Show him in," she said.

Hargreaves nodded and Jack appeared in the doorway a moment later. He glanced around and saw the gathering. "Oh. Ah...."

Violet took a drink from Lila and handed it to Jack. "You're just in time for whatever Cook has whipped up if you'd like to stay. Though I fear you'll be conscripted for our machinations."

His lips twitched and he nodded, handing Hargreaves his coat. He didn't make apologies for showing up and Violet appreciated it. He accepted that she hadn't turned him away and left the awkwardness behind.

"Only home a day and already called to rally round, dear one?" Lila handed Violet a glass with a wink. "I believe we better return to the sea. I suppose some present might object."

"I object, darling," Denny said dryly. "You were gone far too long. None of my pants fit any longer. I cannot survive another season without you and neither can my wardrobe."

Lila made a kissing face towards her husband. "One would think you were a full grown man capable of caring for oneself."

"One would be wrong," Denny replied, as Violet tucked her hand through Jack's arm and pulled him further into the room. Denny grabbed Lila's hand and pulled her down next to him. "I shall hold you to my side whatever it takes."

"Tell us what's wrong," Gwennie said, looking towards Violet, who had invited Jack to sit with her.

"You look smashing, love," Violet told her friend, who had certainly recovered from traveling and gone back to peaches and cream skin, bright eyes, and a steady smirk. Violet glanced around for Victor. "Surely my lazy brother will appear in a moment or two. But we can begin without him." Violet sat on the edge of the Chesterfield. "You must all swear your selves to carry this horrid tale to your graves. Whether the plan goes aright or horribly wrong."

A chorus of promises filled the air. Violet told the tale of Isolde, her fiancé, and what

Violet had seen and heard of the man. While she spoke, describing Danvers's horridness and Isolde's naivety, she could feel Jack's attention on her. It warmed her, and she prayed she wasn't blushing too terribly. Victor appeared during the middle of the tale and let Violet finish.

"How horribly Victorian," Lila said, glancing at the others before she drained her glass.

"I've never met this sister of yours, darling, but she sounds a bit dim."

"She's not dim," Gwennie said, to Violet's surprise. "She's young. I'd have succumbed to the right fairytale at the same age, especially with my aunt's pressure, if not for my elder sister who took me aside and told me to buck up and stand firm."

"You're all young," Jack said, swirling his drink in his glass, "but this is not a fate for your little sister."

"Tell us, Methuselah," Victor countered, as he handed Jack another drink. "What shall we do?"

"Come now," Denny interrupted, tapping off his cigarette. "Vi has a plan. Haven't you, darling?"

Violet shrugged and outlined her thoughts, glancing at Jack when she said they'd need the name of Danvers's mistress. Jack paused, thinking the request over, and then said, "Yes, I should be able to find that out."

"What else do we do?" Victor asked.

"Our time is so limited," Violet said, feeling the worry of it. The wedding was a mere week away. They should have hurried home after they'd gotten their letter. Both Victor and Violet had assumed that Isolde had succumbed to the love-making of some young fellow like herself. Too young to be wed, perhaps, but a story like Denny and Lila's could be happy. "Our best chance is to convince her, only we haven't been close. Why would she let us sway her against her own mother? If we can pick Danvers apart...that might be the surest course. We've already set our man of business to investigating his financials. I have no doubt that his instincts are right. I'm just concerned there isn't time enough."

"Then what shall you do?" Lila asked gently.

"I don't know," Violet admitted. "I don't want to face Isolde a decade from now and admit I knew her life would be terrible. It's never the cads like Danvers who die young. They linger on, tormenting those saddled with their connection."

A luncheon of vichyssoise, fish, and small chocolate cakes followed. It was served as they debated other options, but none of them were quite sure what to do.

"This isn't a problem for our era," Gwennie declared. "That's the issue here. We never expected to face this kind of thing. It was a problem for our grandmothers with their uptight mothers who cared more for money and being settled than they did for happiness."

"Too true, love," Lila said with a sigh. If anything, Lila's family objected for her wishing to marry so young to poor Denny. His good connections and prospects hadn't been enough to sway her mother's worries, and Lila had been forced to throw epic tantrums to get her way. Her parents' concerns had been that she was too young. It was because of those objections that Lila and Denny had waited until after college to wed.

Vi's two female friends swore to drop casual asides to Isolde, making her aware of what Danvers was like, while Jack promised to see if there was anything to be found about Danvers that might scuttle the marriage before it took off.

———

After the others had left, Jack invited Violet to the Criterion and a play for later that week. She accepted with the blush she'd been fighting off all afternoon. "I'll stop by or call if I find anything about Danvers," he said to both Victor and Violet.

Victor stepped away, and Jack's gaze flicked over Violet.

"You can only do what you can, Violet. You might not be able to save your sister if she doesn't wish it."

Violet nodded and let Jack take her hand. He turned her palm over and seemed fascinated by the size of her small white hand against his larger tanned one.

"What happened to your arm?"

The question was so out of the blue that Violet didn't know to what he referred. Jack gently touched her bicep and she glanced at it, noting for the first time the finger-shaped bruises on her skin.

"Ahhh." She looked back to Jack and saw the fire in his gaze. Carefully, she licked her lips.

"Victor?"

She laughed. "Never. I doubt he's noticed yet, or he'd be next to you demanding answers."

"Who?"

"I think..."

"Please?"

The question was so gentle, Violet couldn't deny answer.

"Danvers and I had a rather heated exchange."

Jack nodded, jaw flexing. "I'll be back tomorrow with what I'm able to discover."

Violet nodded. He made his goodbyes and left. The moment the door closed after him,

Victor returned.

"I like him," Victor declared.

"It's moving too fast in my mind," Violet said. "A house party, one casual meeting on a train, and one evening out does not add up to all the places my mind is going."

Victor wrapped his arm around her shoulder. "Oh, darling one, trust me. You've got him well-trapped in your web."

"I don't wish to trap anyone," she said, elbowing him a little.

"It's the only way to catch someone these days, darling. Marriage is for old-fashioned types. If you want to follow the well-trodden path of our ancestors, then you need to lasso your man, or is it hogtie? Is that what those American cowboys do?"

Violet scowled at him and elbowed him once again. "Whatever that is, it sounds quite distasteful. Do not forget, brother of mine, that I am a....what did you call me? A pearl of great price? One such as me does not hogtie a man. We simply flutter our lashes and beckon with our gaze."

Victor's laugh warmed her. "Darling, I was referring to your new, bulging pocketbook, not your intrinsic value."

Violet elbowed her brother a third time before returning to her bedroom and her stolen typewriter. Her story of the ingénue took a sour turn, and Violet knew that it would be a darker tale than she usually wrote. The outcome for the little woman who looked remarkably like their sister, Isolde, was fraught with danger and looked very poor indeed.

CHAPTER SEVEN

The next morning Violet rang up her sister and invited her on a spur of the moment shopping trip. She made a last-minute appointment at the new fashion salon owned by the squire's daughter she'd learned about just before she had left London the last time.

Before long, Violet was gathering up her sister. Isolde gasped when she saw Violet had driven herself.

"You drive?"

"Of course," Violet said. "Victor doesn't let me get away with womanly wiles when he wants to sleep the drive away. I learned quite some time ago, I'm afraid."

"Oh my." Isolde's bright eyes fixed on the car and she mused, "Perhaps I shall learn to drive."

"You should, darling. There's a wonderful freedom in it."

They made their way to the fashion salon and found gowns to stop a clothes monger in her tracks.

"It must be lovely," Isolde said, "to shop without Mother making your choices."

"Dear," Violet said gently, "you can do the same."

"Well, it's important to select the right look to marry Mr. Danvers. He needs a sophisticated woman."

Violet had to hold back a tirade before she brightly replied, "Sweet sister, you are the catch here. He is the lucky one."

"Oh no," Isolde said, shaking her head. "No. Not me."

"Of course you. You're beautiful. You're rich. Your father is an earl. Mr. Danvers is none of those things."

"I'm not nearly as lovely as you," Isolde said, without even an ounce of irony.

"Yes, darling, you are. Of course, you are."

"And I'm not clever like you," Isolde said. She said it with such utter surety that Violet wanted to scream. Just how many times had Lady Eleanor praised Violet to Isolde's detriment?

"Darling, darling, you just left school. You haven't had a chance to study your own interests or discover your passions. It is far too soon to make such judgments."

Isolde smiled at Violet as though she were blind to the obvious and only being kind.

"Why don't you give yourself some more time before you make such big decisions? Push back the wedding date. Travel some with Victor and me. We'd love to take you somewhere exciting and new."

Isolde tucked a loose strand of hair behind her ear. "Did you discover upon cutting your hair that it was so much less weight?"

Violet stared at her sister, who avoided Vi's gaze. "Are you sure you don't wish to push back the date?"

Isolde tucked a lock of hair behind her ear on the opposite side. "It's so much less weight, isn't it? After shearing one's head."

"Yes," Violet said. "It's wonderful to cut off your hair. Perhaps college? I would be happy to pay for you like my aunt paid for me. You don't have to jump into this wedding."

Isolde smiled at Violet, such a sad little expression for what should be a happy movement, and then said, "Isn't that dress just lovely?"

Violet blinked rapidly. "I missed your birthday. Let's try it on you and get it for you. Or something else if we find something that flatters you better."

Isolde nodded in gratitude, but it wasn't for the dress, it was for Violet dropping the subject. They both tried on a series of dresses and both left the shop laden with bags. As they approached the automobile and arranged their bags inside, Violet waited until Isolde was in the vehicle before she shut the door and then turned to her.

Vi had her sister trapped and needed to try one more time. "You are very young."

"Violet..." Isolde's attention was fixed outside the window, but Violet could see the tension through Isolde's slender frame.

"You cannot possibly love Danvers."

"I will come to love him," Isolde said, almost desperately. "He is a good man."

Violet was certain both of those things were untrue, but she could see that all she was doing was distancing herself from her little sister.

"Isolde, I will say this but once and leave you be..." Vi waited until Isolde's gaze turned to hers. "We were never close, but we can be. Victor and I are here for you. Any time, any day. Come to me, and I will help you."

Isolde swallowed and nodded rapidly.

"Before you are married or after, I promise. There are many, many paths before you. All of them can lead to happiness if you're brave enough to follow your heart and trust in your strength."

Isolde nodded again and looked back out the window. Vi took her sister home, consigning her stepmother to all the circles of hell and then returned home to Victor with less hope than she'd had before.

———

Violet dropped her bags in the entrance hall with Hargreaves, leaving him with her coat and hat, then fluffed her hair on the way to the dining room. Jack and Victor were sitting at the table. There was a simple tray of sandwiches, what looked like a carafe of coffee and another of lemonade.

They both stood as she entered, and she announced, "All is lost."

"Lost, is it?"

Violet jumped and realized that her oldest brother had followed her into the dining room.

"Gerald!" Violet said with a gasp. "You startled whatever wits I have to the winds."

He grinned at her and kissed her cheek before pulling out a chair. In his mid-thirties, their brother was a good ten years older than the twins. He managed the earl's estates while spending a good amount of time in London. Like the twins, he had avoided being married thus far, but unlike the twins, Lady Eleanor had never harassed him about his state.

"All is lost?" Victor asked, pouring Violet a glass of lemonade. "How could it be, dear one? We've yet to enact our plan."

"I went rogue," she admitted. "I rang up Isolde and invited her shopping for her birthday. I think that might be the first time I've truly been around Isolde unaccompanied. I...forgive the dramatics, but Isolde is convinced that she has nothing to offer. She is convinced that despite the age difference and the lack of love, Danvers is the best she can attain."

"The devil, you say." Victor swore and cleared his throat. "It's Lady Eleanor."

"Oh certainly," Gerald said. "I'm delighted you two are trying to stick your oar in, but I don't see it being successful. I've tried to convince Isolde otherwise several times yet. She's... intransigent."

"Lady Eleanor has been very clearly tearing Isolde to pieces in order to get her to believe this nonsense."

"It's worse than that, Violet." Jack cleared his throat and pulled out a small black notebook. "I sent my man over to the club this morning. The woman Mr. Danvers was with was Helen Mathers."

"Mathers?" Gerald frowned and seated himself back at his plate. "Not Harry Mathers's daughter? The flighty little blonde one?"

"Just so," Jack stated. "It seems that there was talk for quite a while about them marrying."

"Father can't possibly know that," Victor said.

"I have told Father time and again that this man is a snake in the grass," Gerald stated.

"The problem is that Eleanor's brother says otherwise. Father thinks I'm starting at hares."

Victor moaned. "I stopped by Fredericks's again today. I had to sign a few more things about the house and while I was there, I asked about Danvers too. If he'd found out anything. It seems that no one who knows their business will deal with him."

"So he isn't even rich?"

"Fredericks feels certain that much of his stated wealth is unlikely. He thought I was considering joining one of Danvers's investment schemes despite your objections. He felt that I might be sidestepping you, so Mr. Fredericks did, in fact..."— Victor paused to scowl at Violet— "state I should follow your good advice." Violet laughed at Victor, and he winked at her a moment later. "I was forced to assure Fredericks that I had every intention of letting you be in charge of all the details of my life."

Gerald laughed uproariously at Victor's scowl, but Jack leaned back, eyeing Violet with interest.

"I am letting Fredericks have his head. It's why he wants you to follow my advice. That is beside the point as far as Isolde is concerned." Violet tapped her cheek as she considered their options. "I'm concerned that there is little we can do."

"We will be left with the option to support her once she finally leaves him," Victor said. "I'm sure Lady Eleanor will try to stick her oar in when that day arrives as well."

"She chose far better for herself than for her daughter," Violet said. She rose to pace the dining room, ignoring the sandwiches while the gentlemen watched her.

"You have rather the best chance with her," Gerald told Violet. "She always has looked up to you, you know?"

Violet shook her head and admitted, "I didn't know."

"Our stepmother used to compare Isolde to the ladies around Kennington House since they spent so much time there. But then Isolde would chatter on about you. How lovely you were. Your style. The way you did well in school and out-performed even Victor. Peter and Lionel told Isolde before they went off to war to pay attention to you. That you would look after her when they could not."

Violet had to bite her lip to hold back her tears. She hadn't expected her dead brothers to have said any such things. To refer to *her* as anything other than a silly school girl. Hearing such things made their loss all the more real. Victor cleared his throat, as touched by the sentiment as Violet.

"Yes," Violet said, with a watery choking sound to her

voice. "Well. Now I feel all the more that there must be some way to help Isolde. The poor thing."

Violet listened as Jack recapped what he'd learned. The three men made a list of things to do about Danvers. As they did, Violet considered a course of action that was completely inappropriate. But when Jack and Gerald left, Jack confirming their next date, she escaped to her room. It would be better if no one knew what she was up to.

Violet wrote an anonymous letter to Harry Mathers and Helen Mathers. She then followed those letters up by a letter to Fredericks to do what he could to pull apart the house of cards. She authorized him to spend some of her money without bankrupting her, and she told him to prod Danvers's major investors.

She felt sick when she was done writing the series of instructions and letters, but she would do what was necessary to protect her sister. The biggest problem, she realized as she journaled that evening, wasn't even her actions of the day and the things she'd done, but the fact that she'd allowed her relationship with Isolde to be determined by Vi's stepmother.

What if she'd simply been a better sister? She was disappointed in herself to an extent that was difficult for her to formulate.

Repentance, Vi thought. Repentance and doing far, far better. She didn't just owe it to herself or to Isolde. Vi owed it to the brothers who'd trusted her more than she'd realized. With a heavy heart, she turned to her story, and things continued to worsen for the poor ingénue.

CHAPTER EIGHT

"How can it be the day of the wedding?" Violet demanded. "How can we have failed?"

"I don't know," Victor admitted. "Divorce. Annulment. Something will give eventually, and we'll be at the ready."

"I feel like I have been begging Isolde and begging her, and nothing gives. Did you know she was this stubborn?"

"I'm not surprised," Victor told her as he handed her out of the Silver Ghost, leaving Giles with their bags. They'd stay at Kennington House that night since the wedding festivities would go deep into the evening. "You are stubborn and she aspires to be just like you."

Violet scowled at her brother. "I feel as though it's all my fault. She seems to look up to me, but why? I am such a failure."

Victor kissed the side of her head and held out his arm. They had done everything they could, save kidnapping Isolde and escaping to Greece or America, and now Violet felt as though they certainly needed to do just that. She'd have considered trying it if she thought she could get Isolde away from her mother. But Lady Eleanor seemed to be aware of just how close Violet had come to succeeding time and again.

There was a small church on the property. The wedding would be performed there with those who could be squeezed in. Afterward, there would be a wedding dinner and reception.

They expected the festivities to go well into the evening.

"Stop me from diving too far into my cups," Violet begged.

Victor said, "I thought that you should be the steward of my not getting sloppy drunk instead."

"Perhaps we should just have a little party at the house tomorrow with Lila and Denny and Gwennie and..." She cut off at Jack's name before she softly added, "Jack, and allow ourselves the freedom to drown in those cups."

Victor squeezed her arm and they turned to face Harry Mathers. Violet could hardly believe that he was attending, let alone bringing his daughter. Did he realize the nature of her relationship with his business partner? Violet's letter to him had referred only to the concerns Fredericks had about the investment scheme. Helen's face was pale, her eyes shadowed, and Violet kissed both of her cheeks before she smiled charmingly and stated, "You look just lovely. That shade of pink brings out the creaminess of your skin."

"Oh." Helen licked her trembling lips. "Thank you."

"Do let me introduce you to my friend, John Lexington," Violet told her. "I think you'll find he's quite appealing. I'll find him and introduce you at the party."

They exchanged pleasantries after the introductions.

"You hate John Lexington," Victor accused.

"He's boring, but a good man. Helen needs someone who would cherish her after that idiot Danvers."

The twins made their way through the crowd, and Violet kept her gaze peeled for their sister. She hadn't yet made an appearance and must have decided to only appear at the end of the aisle. There was no question she'd look like an angel.

"I...think I'll just check on Isolde. Last words of love and all that," Violet murmured.

Victor grabbed her arm and shook his head as they rounded the corner of the house.

They halted suddenly. Markus Kennington and Mr. Gulliver had Danvers cornered against the side of the house, and the furious whispering between them was so clearly enraged that Violet wasn't quite sure what to do.

"Victor?" She questioned quietly, then stumbled back when Markus Kennington shoved Danvers against the side of the house.

Victor demanded, "What's all this then?"

"You should have let Markus have at Danvers," Violet whispered. "Maybe if he gets the tar beat out of him, he won't be able to marry Isolde."

"Too late, love. And not in front of you." Victor stepped forward, telling Violet to stay, and was rounded on, not by Markus Kennington, but by Danvers.

"Go, Violet," Victor urged. Reluctant to leave her brother, still she hurried away. Once inside the house, she had to bully her way past the butler and had no doubt that he'd been set to turn her away. He tried politely, but she plowed right through, leaving him with the choice of bodily removing her or stepping aside.

The stairs up to the room that had been set aside for the bride were deserted, and outside the door, a maid stood with a panicked expression on her face. She held a tray and Violet took it from her, ignoring the sounds of shouting that were coming from inside of the room.

Warmed by the sound of an enraged stepmother, Violet did not knock; she simply swung the door open after shooing the maid away.

Lady Eleanor spun with fire in her gaze, and when she saw Violet, she shrieked, "You!

This is all your fault!"

Violet calmly set the tray down and faced the weeping Isolde.

"I cannot do it, Mama," Isolde begged. "I cannot."

"You think I'll allow you to throw away all I've crafted for you? All of my hard work?

For what? An idiotic fairytale? Isolde, absolutely not."

Violet had to bite her lip to keep from standing up for Isolde. It was far past time that

Isolde spoke for herself.

"I won't marry him," Isolde said.

"You will!"

"You cannot make me say the words," Isolde said flatly. "This isn't medieval times, Mama. No, I won't."

Lady Eleanor huffed. She was breathing so heavily, Violet thought her stepmother might faint.

"Then what will you do? If you think your father and I will support you in this madness, in this...travesty, you are wrong!"

"Vi said she'd pay for my school. I will go to school. Perhaps I shall work," Isolde said.

Her voice was quiet, but there was no give in it. Violet wanted to cheer.

Lady Eleanor's gaze narrowed and she turned to Violet. Before she could speak, Isolde turned her mother back to face her.

"Enough, Mama. I told you I won't do it, and I won't. You can tell Papa or I shall, but this will not happen."

"If you think that I will make your bed for you, you are very wrong." Lady Eleanor spun on Violet. "I hope you're prepared to support your sister for the entirety of her life because you can be assured that your father and I will not."

Violet cleared her throat and said evenly, "I am assured that Father would do just that.

However, Victor and I would welcome Isolde after she is done with school." "And you! I have heard of your shenanigans."

"Excuse me?" Violet asked silkily.

"You are still seeing a...a...detective. Do you think your father will allow that?"

"After allowing Danvers? I think so." Violet still hadn't explained just who Jack Wakefield was or why he was so very eligible, and she did not intend on making those explanations.

Violet rang the bell. "I'll send for Papa, shall I? Try to put on a trifle more cheerful air, darling. I assure you that Father will support you going to school. He certainly did for me. It's expected these days, you know. Only the most archaic of parents want to see their children married off before they've even caught their breath from the schoolroom."

The next moment, Lady Eleanor slammed the door on her way out, and Isolde burst into tears.

"Hallelujah, my sister!" Violet said. "I am so proud!"

Isolde tears turned to laughter. "I..."

"Don't worry, darling. You were living in a world of horror, avoiding specters that only exist in Lady Eleanor's fantasy."

The maid arrived and was sent after the earl while Violet helped Isolde take off the wedding gear. Vi tossed Isolde's dress on the bed and proceeded to pack her trunk. A thought occurred to her and she rang the bell again, sending another maid after Victor and a glass of scotch.

"What have I done?" Isolde moaned while Violet packed Isolde's trunks for her.

"Just what you should have. I promise you, your mother will come around, and the rest of us have been waiting for this moment. How brave you are to end it before you marry the fellow and have to go through the scandal of divorce. I assure you, you would have."

Violet considered again and sent a third maid after Lila and Gwennie. Her sister needed cheering and Lila, combined with enough alcohol, would get Isolde happy. Victor would ensure the trunks made their way to the Silver Ghost, and Violet would write a letter to Jack. They'd sweep Isolde to... anywhere else. He would understand, wouldn't he?

Violet winced inside as she realized just how painful it would be to leave Jack. She might have been trying to keep her mind from leaping ahead, but she'd been failing. The idea of a relationship with him had burrowed into her heart.

Before Violet was half-done packing for Isolde, there was a knock on her door and Gwennie and Lila swept in. Lila took in the sight of Isolde in a regular dress, weeping into her scotch while Violet packed her bags and said, "Praise be. What do we need?"

"Victor is going to need help with these trunks if we want to escape before most everyone realizes what is afoot. Perhaps Denny?"

"I left him smoking with John Davies."

"Lovely, John will surely be on our side. Gwennie, would you?"

Gwen nodded and hurried out the bedroom door while Lila knelt in front of Isolde and told her all the reasons she was making the right decision.

Victor arrived next, saw what was happening in a glance, and said, "Brava, Isolde! Has anyone told Father yet?"

Violet shook her head. She was fighting her need for precision with the need to move quickly.

Lila understood when she caught Violet carefully folding a dress. "Darling," Lila said, taking the dress from Violet. "You can afford a maid to press this dress now." To Victor, Lila said, "I'll help Vi and we'll keep a hand on Isolde's bravery. We need these bags to the car and the car capable of leaving quickly."

"I'll get the car outside of the house," Victor said. "I'm proud of you, Isolde."

"I should have done it sooner," she said with tears. "Even last night would have been better. How did I get here?"

"We're all weak in the face of our elders," Gwennie told her. "This will be an exciting tale when you're at college."

"Better now, darling, than after," Victor agreed, squeezing Isolde's shoulder. "There is always worse timing. There is no question that Danvers is an out and out bounder. We have been trying to find proof since we realized who he was to pull apart his lies, but we simply didn't have the time."

"Get to it, Victor," Violet said, pushing him gently towards the door. "I don't trust Lady

Eleanor or Danvers enough to not feel as though this isn't a race."

"On it, dear one," he said.

CHAPTER NINE

A good half hour had passed since Victor left, and still no Father. Violet finally pulled Lila to the door and said, "I will find Father myself. You get her to the car the moment Victor returns. I'll meet you there."

Lila nodded and Violet hurried through the halls of Kennington House. She hadn't spent months at a time here as Isolde had, but Vi had been there often enough to find the bedroom always assigned to her father.

It was empty, so she considered for a moment and then hurried down to the library. It would be just like Papa to be having a cigar with Eleanor's brother up until he absolutely had to appear. People were still arriving, but they'd be seated by ushers and he'd have to greet them after the wedding.

The hall outside of the library was empty. Violet knocked on the library door and there was no answer. She almost left to pursue her father elsewhere, except...it was just *so* like him to be having a secret cigar. She pushed the door open and saw that the French doors to the back garden were open. It was possible to make out the shapes of those who were walking across the lawns towards the little church. Most of the guests would have to appear just for the afterwedding party given the size of the chapel, but she still saw Mr. Gulliver talking to Mr. Higgins and Mr. Mathers. They didn't look very happy. It wasn't their wedding though, was it? Why should they be all smiles?

She stepped forward, intending to look for her father further through the French doors. Perhaps Father was hiding in the shadows or on the side of the house? It was a rather hot day for spring; the shade on the side of the house was appealing.

Violet saw the hand first. It was flung so casually out, giant rings on a few fingers. She frowned and stepped further forward.

The slick backed hair was the next thing she noted. It had been disturbed and flopped about in glued together hunks. It was so odd to see the effect of brilliantine in that manner.

It was only then that she noticed the pool of blood. The horribly squashed skull. The terrible result of a candlestick on the groom. She whimpered just a little, turning to run.

Only firming her will, Violet glanced back and examined the scene further. A candlestick flung to the floor near the corpse, the dead Danvers, a bit of a ruckus with scattered papers and an overturned chair, but not enough—perhaps—to draw the attention of the servants.

Especially if the first, terrible blow stopped Danvers from crying out for help. She swallowed, regretted that choice immediately and knew that what she wanted more than anything was Jack, Victor, and her father. To her shock, she realized she wanted them in that order.

Slowly, she turned the latch on the French doors, rang the bell for a servant, and then left the library, shutting the door behind her. She turned the lock as she did so to prevent anyone from entering. She wasn't sure just what Jack or his peers at Scotland Yard would need to be preserved, but she was determined to do what she could.

Her hands were shaking and she was barely choking back hysterics when the butler who'd attempted to head her off not so long before arrived. He scowled at her, and she swallowed on a dry throat.

"I'm afraid there's been a terrible accident." Her voice was shaking, but she felt that by not shrieking down the house, she was showing more fortitude than many could have mustered.

"An accident, miss?"

"You need to call for Scotland Yard. Ask for Mr. Hamilton Barnes. Tell him there has been a murder."

"A murder." The butler sounded disbelieving and Violet's eyes flashed.

The shaking in her hands stopped as her fury escalated. "A murder. Now. You may seek your master after you have made the necessary contact."

Violet could see that the butler wanted to object, and she was overstepping demanding Scotland Yard when she wasn't even a denizen of the house, but she *knew* what she had seen.

Violet held up her hand to stave off his objections. "Mr. Morton, I suggest you do as I command." She was wearing the persona of an earl's daughter. One she didn't like to put on very often, but she could be far more imperious with the lift of her nose and the turn of her head than he was capable of handling.

He opened his mouth to object, and she lifted a solitary brow and crossed her arms over her chest. He didn't contain his objections, but he did as she demanded and rang up Scotland Yard.

"May I get my master now?" The sarcasm was not lost on

Violet, but what cared she for his objections? She nodded once and said, "Send for the *earl* as well."

The butler scurried away. Violet had no doubt that he was heading for Markus Kennington, Lady Eleanor's eldest brother.

And, hadn't Violet just seen him arguing with Mr. Danvers? She had.

"Vi? What are you doing here, darling? I thought we were to be off with Isolde before our escape plans are scuppered."

Violet gasped and hurried down the hall and threw herself into Victor's arms. "He's dead!" The safety of her brother was all she needed to feel her clawed together composure slip.

"What's this now?"

"I was looking for Father and I...I...he's dead."

"Father?" Victor gaped at her and she shook her head frantically.

"No! Thank goodness! Danvers! He's dead. Someone... quite...." Violet felt the horror of it all once again in the safety of Victor's protection and pulled back. "Someone quite crushed his head."

Victor's mouth was agape, but he tucked Violet close to him just as Markus Kennington and their father rushed into the hall.

"What's this madness?" Kennington demanded. "You sent for Scotland Yard? What the devil! There's a wedding afoot."

"Not any longer," Violet replied calmly.

"What has happened, little one? Morton, you're claiming there was a murder. It cannot be so, can it?"

"There's no question," Violet told her father and shivered as the recollection assaulted her once again. "It is very clearly murder, and Danvers is very clearly dead."

Father nodded. "Dead is he?" The question was quizzical and he seemed no more concerned about the death of his future son-in-law as he would be over an old horse. "Your butler already called the yard, Kennington. Nothing to do but wait, I'm afraid."

"Did you send for Jack?" Victor whispered.

Violet shook her head and murmured, "I told them to ask for Mr. Barnes."

"Clever girl," Victor said. "Morton, some tea for my sister with a generous splash of something stronger."

The butler's face had become impassive in the view of his master, but he nodded once and said, "Of course, sir."

"Are we just going to believe her?" Kennington demanded.

"Course we will," Father said. "She's hardly a ninny."

"She is a female." Kennington scowled at Father, at Violet, and then back to Father.

"She's got eyes, hasn't she? Vi ain't no wilter. If she says the fella's dead, he's dead. If she says it's murder, it's murder. Don't be daft in the head, Kennington."

Violet leaned heavily into Victor. The sheer idea of the crime being anything other than murder was bringing back what she'd seen. She shuddered again and Victor said, "Father, Vi needs..."

"Course, course," Father said. "The parlor here. It's got to be open, ain't it? With the wedding nonsense?"

Kennington would have objected, but before he could, Father flung the door open and the waiting for Scotland Yard to arrive began.

———

The drive from London to Kennington House wasn't long. Once you got outside the city, it was a mere hour into the countryside. The journey out of the city could be fraught with frustration, but Barnes made good time and appeared by the time Victor had pushed Violet into drinking her scotch and tea and then pushed her into eating a sandwich. He kept refilling her teacup, and the burning in her nose and throat became a constant semi-enjoyable pain.

Victor hadn't allowed anyone to pressure her for details but drew them from her himself in a way that lessened the pain of the recollection. He didn't leave her other than to whisper to Father about Isolde, who nodded and disappeared up the stairs to talk to the daughter who had abandoned her wedding plans before her groom had been killed.

Victor then stood guard over her while others tried to dig. Kennington had disappeared to delay the guests from leaving, and Lady Eleanor appeared only to be unceremoniously refused entrance.

After that, Victor and Violet were left alone in silence. They sat on yet another Chesterfield, side-by-side as they always did. Her head was on his shoulder, and she was trying very hard not to think of what she'd seen.

"I didn't realize what a gift it was not to see Aunt Agatha..."

"Don't think of it," Victor told Vi, refilling her teacup with the decanter of scotch. She shivered and nodded, laying her head back on his shoulder until he lifted her teacup to her mouth.

"Do you suppose we're suspects?" Violet asked a few minutes later. "Jack knows we hated Danvers and were trying to ruin the wedding."

"I doubt very much that you will be, love," Victor said. "Drink your tea now."

Violet sat up and turned on him. "Tea?" she scoffed. "It was barely tea before you started refilling it."

Victor grinned without a smidgen of repentance and said, "I suppose that party we were going to have isn't quite the thing, now."

The tenor of the question struck Violet as ridiculous and she broke into giggles. She was still laughing several minutes later and wiping her eyes with Victor's handkerchief when Jack and Mr. Barnes entered the parlor.

"Is she weeping?"

Violet giggled and said, "Hullo there, good sir!"

"I suspect I pushed too much scotch into her," Victor said staidly, glancing down at the giggling, shivering, and weeping Violet. "I take full responsibility."

"What happened?" Jack demanded as Violet sniffled and then giggled a little more.

"I didn't realize how enjoyable the burn of scotch could be," Vi told Jack. "Do you like it?"

Her voice was high-pitched and cheery even as she shivered again and wiped away a tear.

Victor recapped the events while Violet tried and failed to get herself into control. Once Victor had done, Jack squatted down in front of Vi and said, "Are you all right?"

"You have rather remarkable eyes, did you know?"

Victor's snort seemed to make Jack blush. Vi grinned in delight at the slight rosy tone to his cheeks. He wasn't so large while he was before her like this. Well, he was, but he didn't make her feel quite so small when he wasn't towering over her. She discovered that his effect on her had no change.

"Don't be shy," Vi told him. "Not everyone has nice eyes, you know." Her tone was very serious as she leaned in and whispered, "Lady Eleanor's are rather faded and watery."

Jack's lips twitched and he said, "I know where they live, Barnes. I think Victor better get Violet home. We can question them after Violet has a nap and perhaps another sandwich to sop up all the booze Victor poured into her."

Violet shivered again, a tear sneaking out of her eye, "It was awful."

"You see..." Victor said, looking helplessly at Violet as she shivered once again, breaking into a new case of gooseflesh. "I can't..."

Violet's lower lip quivered and she said, "I'm sorry. I'm so sorry. I just keep...I just keep seeing it. Vic didn't let me see Aunt Aggie." Violet was crying fully then and Jack cleared his throat. "I didn't like it at the time, but now..."

"I see..." Jack said, clapping a hand on Victor's shoulder.

"I had to," Victor said.

"Had to what?" Vi asked glancing between the three of them, who were all looking at her rather seriously.

"It didn't stop her crying though, did it?" Barnes shook his head and said, "We can't protect them from everything."

Victor glanced back at Violet and swore, "But damned if I won't try. Not sure she'll let me take her home without Isolde though. I don't suppose I can have her too? She can't have done this."

"Not if the murder is as you say," Jack said. "It would have to be someone larger than either Violet or Isolde."

"Couldn't be Isolde," Violet told them all. "Doubt she was alone since the moment she woke." Violet suddenly yawned, placing a hand over her mouth, but the yawn shook her whole body. "Shouldn't be happy. I'm not happy. But it's better he's gone. Better for Isolde. Solves a lot of the trouble for her. I keep seeing it."

"Don't think of it," Victor and Jack said in unison.

Vi yawned again and shivered, not even noticing when another tear fell. Jack stood and pulled Violet up. "Get your other sister, Victor. Take them both to your house and don't leave. We'll be by."

Victor nodded and Violet found herself alone with Jack once again, being bundled into the back of the Silver Ghost.

"Don't leave me," she begged. She dared to lay her head on his shoulder while he sat next to her. Not his shoulder. He was too large for that. This monstrous thing under her cheek was his arm. She reached her hand, still trembling, up to touch it and then yawned again. "You won't go?"

"Not until Victor is here."

Violet glanced out the window, seeing Markus Kennington and his cousin watching from an upper window. She shivered yet again. But this time it wasn't memories that were assaulting her. It was the realization that someone she knew had murdered that bounder, Danvers.

CHAPTER TEN

Violet fell asleep in the automobile on the way back to their house, but her dreams were fraught with searching for the people she loved and never quite finding them.

"I'm right here, luv," Victor said soothingly one of the times she woke herself asking for him, but when she slipped back into sleep, he was gone again. Whatever would she do without him? She couldn't imagine a future where he wasn't a daily part of it. Even at college, they'd seen each other so often they might as well have been in the same houses.

"Is she always this melancholy when she's in her cups?" Isolde's voice cut through Violet's fitful sleeping, and she sat up for a moment before turning towards Victor and snuggling into his side.

"It isn't the scotch," Victor said.

"It was awful," she murmured into his shoulder, wishing she could slip deeply into sleep instead of waking and falling back asleep as she was doing.

"I know, darling. Don't think of it."

"I can't make it stop," she whispered as the dream claimed her again.

The motion of the automobile ceased. She woke when Victor pulled her from the car, and she found herself in his arms.

"Do you remember that time I fell from the tree?" she asked in a sleep-thickened voice.

"Carried you like this then, too."

"Don't go?" she asked. It was her dreams speaking, and she was asleep on his shoulder again before he could answer.

When she woke later that evening, it was to Beatrice gently shaking her shoulder.

"M'lady," Beatrice said quietly. "M'lady. Dinner is to be served and Mr. Wakefield and Mr. Barnes are here to speak with the household."

Violet shoved off her eye mask and found she'd been bundled into her bed in her dress without her shoes, jewelry, or hairpiece. Someone had taken care to put her eye mask on to block out the sun, but it was long gone now.

"What time is it?"

"Near seven, m'lady."

Violet pushed back her hair and asked, "How long do I have?"

"As long as you need, m'lady. They all said so."

Violet slowly stood. She didn't feel so much sick to her stomach as sick to her heart. She took the aspirin that Beatrice had ready, along with Giles's concoction, hurried it all down, and decided to take them at their word.

Beatrice drew a bath for her while she brushed her teeth. A quick bath later, and Violet pulled on her most comfortable dress and an oversized sweater. She didn't feel up to bothering with makeup except for a little color on her lips. If this thing between her and Jack continued, he'd have to discover she had a few freckles on her nose.

They had gathered around the dining table once again. The cook had been informed they intended to bring a few friends home, but not to put forth such a great effort. So they didn't have more than the simple repast they would normally have requested.

Violet crossed immediately to Isolde, who was a pale sort of green, and hugged her tight. "Are you all right?"

"Are you?" Isolde's bright blue eyes searched Vi's face. She nodded and they hugged once again.

Violet carefully pushed back one of Isolde's loose curls. "I know this is awful right now, luv, but I am still proud of you."

She turned to the rest of the room and found that the gentlemen had stood and were watching the interaction between the sisters.

Jack was standing next to his friend and former commander, Mr. Barnes. They both had the sort of alert, hunting look that Violet imagined had been normal for them during the war.

"There is food," Victor said, as he rubbed the back of his neck. "Perhaps we might eat and discuss this as though it were a sort of intellectual problem."

"Rather than the murder of Isolde's bounder betrothed?" Violet asked.

Mr. Barnes said, "This is all very....inappropriate. We shouldn't be consorting with..."

"Suspects?" Isolde looked weepy, and Mr. Barnes didn't answer her. She wasn't, however, incorrect.

"Do it anyway, old man," Victor said, with that edge of the lion, the earl's son, in his tone. He was in full protective mode with both of his younger sisters present and upset. "I won't have you dragging off my sisters to badger them with questions, not without me there."

"Victor..." Violet started, but he shook his head.

"Not today, Vi."

"Violet and Isolde couldn't have killed him. Given the amount of damage and the size of

Danvers, they wouldn't have been physically strong enough. It was but a single blow that ended him," Jack said. "And Victor was seen during the likeliest window of when it could have occurred."

Mr. Barnes searched all their faces and then nodded once.

"Cook made beef stew and Yorkshire pudding," Victor said, interrupting smoothly, once more back to his usual calm. "Not very elegant, I'm afraid, but it'll warm our bones."

The dinner was served with ginger beer. Violet grinned at her glass as she accepted it from Hargreaves, well aware that the drink had been selected because Victor saw the pain behind her eyes. Giles and Hargreaves worked together to serve the dinner and Mr. Barnes kept a notepad next to his plate, making notes as they discussed the history of one Mr. Carlton Danvers.

"How did you meet him?" Violet asked Isolde.

"Mama, of course." Isolde paused and then explained, "Uncle Kennington and Mama were rather good friends with him before I was ever introduced. Before I was even out of the schoolroom, Mama talked to me about being secure and Mr. Danvers's name came up again and again. How he wasn't quite the thing in looks, but such a good man. Such a steady man. A safe refuge for a flighty, romantic thing like me. Mama made it seem as though…" Isolde didn't finish her thought, but Violet could imagine.

Lady Eleanor had pressured her daughter from the school-room, introduced them as a fate already accomplished, an established arrangement, and Isolde hadn't found the gump-tion to kick up a fuss.

Father said he'd try to stop things, but what if his little asides had been laughed off by

Lady Eleanor? Isolde may have been entirely unaware that

Father objected, with his manner of protesting. He was so lackadaisical about things, and one had to be quite familiar with him to be aware of when he was unhappy. Would it be so surprising if Isolde wasn't privy to that trait?

"I think we see," Mr. Barnes said gently. "Were you aware of any enemies?"

Isolde shook her head. "Mama kept me focused on shopping and furniture. I just tried to enjoy the jewelry and not think too far ahead."

Victor set his drink down with a rather forceful click, but he did nothing more than cross his finger in front of him.

Violet despised her next question, but it had to be asked. "What do you know of Helen Mathers?"

Isolde glanced at Violet and blushed brightly enough that Violet thought her innocent sister may be rather aware of more than Violet would have guessed.

"She distracted him from me, didn't she?"

Victor's laugh was approving while Barnes looked on confused.

"The lady friend," Jack said under his breath, and clarity crossed Barnes's expression.

He'd clearly heard enough to know of her existence.

"What do you know of the son?" Barnes asked.

Isolde glanced at the table and blushed. She didn't quite meet their eyes and Violet frowned. That was the look of a girl who had been pushed.

"Did he express an interest in you?" Violet's tone was bright, as though the idea didn't infuriate her.

Isolde nodded just a little.

Vi's anger was mounting, and she had to move her shaking fingers into her lap so Isolde didn't see her reaction. The table was awkwardly silent as everyone tried to contain reactions to what Isolde had experienced. Isolde didn't see it because she was hiding her gaze.

Violet pressed her lips tightly together and then was unable to hold back. "Isolde, you cannot stop interest others might have in you. You cannot stop someone looking at you and thinking you are lovely. You are." Violet reached over and took Isolde's hand. "You cannot make a man keep his comments, gaze, or hands to himself. But if he does not, it is *not* your fault."

Isolde's gaze lifted to Violet and the two sisters understood each other in a way that the men at the table could not.

"I, however, can," Victor said. "If you need me..."

Violet's laugh was gentle but ungiving when she said, "You won't always be there, dear brother. If only all men were like you, then Isolde and I would never need to worry our pretty little heads over it."

Violet's mocking tone made everyone relax, so she squeezed Isolde's hand and took a sip of her drink before changing the subject. "Isolde, what about those business partners. Gulliver and Higgins?"

"I only ever regularly met Uncle Kennington and Mr. Mathers. Mr. Mathers and Mr.

Danvers had done business for quite some time, I believe. Uncle Kennington and Norman Kennington only invested in the last year or two. They never really discussed business around me. Or anything really. We'd just eat and see a play, and I'd be delivered home. It was all very..."

Again Isolde's manners prevented her from expressing her real feelings, but Violet could imagine. Uncomfortable? A terrible foreshadowing of the future laid out for her? Vi made a mental note to talk to Victor about taking Isolde away as soon as this case was resolved. A little travel, school in the fall, a new step forward—perhaps her sister would learn to craft her own life.

The questions Isolde answered filled out the picture that Mr. Danvers was a snake in the grass, Lady Eleanor an idiot woman who'd focused only on the piles of purported bullion, and the motives of the killer were still amorphous. It wasn't that they didn't exist, it was that none of the possible motives took shape with any clarity.

Isolde excused herself when the questions were finished, and Violet gazed after her sister. She was tempted to follow, but a glance at Jack and the slight shake of his head told her that they weren't finished questioning the twins.

Violet rang the bell for Hargreaves and had him send Beatrice to care for Isolde while the rest of them adjourned to the library.

Victor seated Violet in a chair near the fire, and the others joined her while Victor requested a coffee tray. Violet murmured a request for a mix of chamomile and mint tea, and his mouth tightened as he nodded. He knew that was the drink of choice when she didn't feel quite the thing.

"What a dashed mess!" Victor said, shoving his legs out before him and steepling his fingers. "By Jove, I won't pretend to be sorry it happened. Thank god it did!"

"Where were you in the hours before?"

Victor answered even though it seemed Jack and Mr. Barnes had a pretty good idea. Violet curled her legs under her and leaned her temple on her fingers in a fruitless attempt to push back the pain in her head.

"Vi and I arrived together. We left Giles with the automobile. The wedding was scheduled for 10:00 a.m., but we'd gotten there early since Vi wanted to love on Isolde a little. Let the dear thing know that we loved her even though we had tried to talk her out of the day. It was our attempt to form a bridge to see Isolde through after the wedding. So she'd feel safe coming to us if she needed to."

"She seems the type to put on a brave face and square her shoulders."

Victor nodded, displeased at the thought, before continu-ing. "It was around 9:00 a.m.

when we made our way to the house. On the way, we saw Markus Kennington and Mr. Gulliver in quite an argument with Danvers. I sent Vi to our sister and remained behind."

"What happened?"

"They walked it off, each of them taking off in a different direction. Our presence had burst whatever that argument was about."

"Did you see many of the guests?" Barnes asked.

Victor considered before listing names. He suddenly turned to Vi. "Mathers. He and his girl were there at the wedding. She didn't look well."

Violet nodded. "Oh yes...I saw him and Higgins and Gulliver too. Right before I noticed the body. They were on the lawn through the French doors." "Did you notice anyone else at that moment?"

Violet shook her head apologetically.

"The..." Barnes glanced at Violet and then said quietly. "It is doubtful that any regularsized woman would be strong enough to commit this crime."

Violet shuddered and closed her eyes.

"Don't think of it," Victor told Vi, and she tried to smile for him.

Hargreaves appeared with the tray. She pushed herself forward to pour for everyone, but Victor commanded her back, handing her a cup first and then pouring coffee for the others.

"You're an excellent hostess, brother." Vi smiled into her tea. His smirk told her he wasn't bothered.

He'd made it sweet and lemony, and it helped settle her stomach, especially after the ginger beer. She had mostly pulled apart the Yorkshire pudding and shuffled the stew around her dish at dinner.

"From what we can tell, all of the major investors in Danvers's scheme were in attendance early, along with your family."

"What are you thinking?" Vi hated the realization that, once again, her family were the main murder suspects.

They didn't answer her, finishing their coffee instead until the men made their excuses.

Barnes and Victor stepped into the hall while Jack squatted in front of her once again.

"You seem fragile."

"It won't last," she promised. "Aunt Agatha, after she was cleaned up, that was the only body I can remember seeing. The way..." Violet's eyes filled with tears. "How did you survive the war?"

He didn't lose sympathy for her when she asked the question. Not even though her trial had been so much less harrowing than his had.

"The things men do to each other can be awful. The things men do *for* each other can be wonderful. I wasn't in the trenches, thank god, but I saw men throw themselves over the body of a friend, one life for another. The good things aren't exclusive to war heroism, either. People are heroic and kind and beautiful every day. Focus on those things and these megrims will fade."

Violet hoped it was true. Maybe at that moment merely because he did, she believed it, but she would cling to the idea all the same.

"I'll check on you tomorrow." He pressed her hand and left her with her cooled tea. That hadn't been a question, and it had been a little proprietary. Her imagination took momentary flight, and she smiled into her tea. Maybe it was better to focus on the little goodnesses of life and turn the big, horrible things over to God, fate, and the universe.

CHAPTER ELEVEN

The world was a better place when Violet woke. The most likely reason was because her head no longer had a drummer boy banging away inside. She dressed with more care than usual because the process of choosing a dress and applying her makeup gave her something to focus on besides the day before.

What was happening with her father? Her brother, Gerald? Had Lady Eleanor forgiven Isolde in the light of her betrothed's death or would there be recriminations and derision over the course of the day? Violet dabbed a light red on her lips and examined her powder. She was still a bit pale, but she'd have to do.

She put her makeup carefully away, took off her kimono and sprayed herself with perfume before she put on the light blue dress. It set off the color of her skin and hair. She finished with a simple cameo at her neck and her hair tucked back with a plain comb. She looked fashionable enough but not bright. She examined the dress, considered the death the day before, and exchanged her dress for a dark grey one instead, with a dropped waistline and pleated skirt.

She made her way to Isolde's room and found the girl. With dark circles under her eyes and her normally pale complexion still paler, Isolde could have been confused for a ghost.

"Cheer up, cheerio," Vi told her sister. "You'll feel better after some food and tea."

Violet pushed her sister through dressing, putting the scattering of Isolde's possessions away as her sister put on a black dress and said, "I suppose I'd better appear to be mourning."

Violet didn't disagree, but she said, "Anyone with half a wit will know you escaped, my love. But putting on the black garb is the best idea. You can keep with it until we take you out of England and then drop the act once the fervor dies down. You can be a bright young thing again, slip into college, and it'll all fade with the perfecting of your French and literature."

Isolde brightened at the idea. "Where shall we go? I have always wanted to visit Bruges, Belgium. My friend, Lisbeth, went. She said she's never seen anything more beautiful."

"Certainly there," Violet agreed without a thought and finished putting Isolde's things away.

The room was tidied, her sister was wan and beautiful in black, and the dark circles under her eyes had been masked with powder. They went down to the breakfast room together and found Victor sitting with Jack and Gerald.

"Isolde, dear." Gerald held his arms out to her, and she kissed each cheek and let him settle her, making a plate for her while she tried to drink her tea.

Violet's greeting from her brother was less enthusiastic, so she made herself a plate and didn't fight the urge to seat herself next to Jack for breakfast.

"You seem to be endlessly feeding me," he murmured.

Victor's laugh distracted Jack from Vi's blush, and she spread marmalade over her toast as Jack admitted, "I wanted to ensure all was well here."

"Who besides me is without an alibi?" Victor asked idly.

"I am," Gerald said. "And I'd have liked to kill the blighter."

Isolde's shocked glance had Gerald holding up his hands and admitting, "I didn't of course, love. Of course, I didn't. I came by to let Wakefield here know that there's a bit of a tizzy happening at Kennington house. Not sure of the details. Everyone becomes silent as monks when I enter. But a lot of hissing and bywords. Muttering and dire looks. You'd think someone was at death's door instead of a blighter we hardly liked already gone."

"Hardly liked." Isolde's offense at Gerald's opinion of her fiancé made Vi's lips twitch, so she sipped her coffee to hide her reaction.

"You knew I didn't like him, Isolde. Don't pretend to be surprised now. Is there tea?"

Gerald demanded. "What's wrong with a good cuppa?"

"Vi and I adjusted to coffee in Italy, boyo." Victor nodded to Hargreaves, who disappeared from his post near the door. The household had only the cook, the butler, Beatrice, and Giles. The servants tended to do quite a bit of double duty when it came to things like this.

They should, Vi thought, probably hire at least one more daily.

"Violet says we can go to Bruges," Isolde told Victor.

His gaze flicked to Vi's, who nodded once, but she noticed Jack's gaze had narrowed on her face. She wasn't quite sure what to do. Isolde needed someone to take her out of the country and distract her. Who else could do it?

"Be good for you to get out of the way until things die

down," Gerald said with a glance between Jack and Violet. Her eldest brother didn't look disapproving. More contemplative.

"After the killer is found, I'm afraid. At least for the gentlemen." It was Jack who cut in and Violet prevented a sigh of relief. She wanted to go to Bruges...just not without Jack. When had this happened to her?

"A *few* weeks in Belgium will be just the thing before college, Isolde," Violet reminded her. "College will shake off this temporary madness, give you a safe place to provide you some distance and help you find your own wants. If you wish to wed and have children..."

"I..." She looked as though it was hard to say and then her mouth firmed and she admitted, "It's always what I wanted."

"Then you can do so," Violet said calmly, "to a man you actually wish to spend your days with."

"Mother says you are too mannish to marry," Isolde told Violet. "Do you not wish to marry?"

Violet snorted before she admitted, "Perhaps. I have had offers, but I have no desire to marry for the sake of the institution. For love, I'd marry for that."

"Love," Gerald repeated. "Women are all the same."

"Don't you believe in love, old man?" Victor leaned back and crossed his leg, waiting for Gerald to reply.

"On occasion," Gerald said. "Less on days like the last few."

"You had better marry," Victor told Gerald strictly. "I don't want that title saddled on me, old boy. If you can't find love, find someone fun, have a kid or two and go back to your shooting or whatever it is that you like."

"Managing the estates is work, Victor," Violet told her brother. "It isn't as though Gerald is the layabout you are."

"That is exactly the problem I am referring to, darling one. Save me, Gerald. Save me from the title and the respon-

sibility. Better yet, save Violet. She'll do it for me, you know.
She doesn't deserve such a fate."

"Siblings, please," Jack said. "I have been conscripted and
must be about my day. No leaving London until you're cleared
to go."

They all nodded, and Violet walked him to the door.

"I'd still like to have dinner and the play. If your mother
doesn't object."

Violet barely held back the derisive snort that comment
deserved. "Her taste in sons-inlaw is not one I endorse."

Jack shifted just a little closer. He didn't cross any proprietary lines, but his bulk made Violet feel safe once again.
With Jack, who wouldn't feel safe?

"Keep close to Victor until the fiend is caught. Isolde *and*
yourself."

Violet nodded and realized she should check on Lady
Eleanor and Father. She should do it that day, but there was
something else that had been growing in her mind since she'd
woken, and she needed to bare her soul.

"May I speak with you for a few moments?"

Jack nodded and followed her into the parlor. "I had
forgotten what I had done."

His gaze went from inquisitive to serious as she started to
pace, stopping here and there to straighten a knick-knack or a
pillow.

"What did you do?" he asked after she'd straightened one
of the pillows twice.

"I...when..." Violet's mouth pursed, then she nibbled on
her lower lip. "I couldn't abide Danvers. Especially after he
manhandled me as he did. I could see Isolde's future, and it
was full of far worse than a bruise on an arm."

Jack nodded and didn't speak. The silence tugged at Violet
until she pressed shaking fingers to her mouth and said, "I
knew from Fredericks that Danvers's investments were very

unlikely to be sound. I knew a few names of the investors. I
had Fredericks approach them. I wrote concerned letters
myself. To Harry and Helen Mathers. I...Jack..." She sat near
him on the edge of the seat. "I told Fredericks to spend what
he needed of my money to tug at the scheme. To see if he
could make it fall apart. If Danvers was proven to be poor,
Lady Eleanor would *delay* the wedding and then later cancel
it. I knew she would. I...think it must all come back to me.
This murder...it's my fault."

Violet was fully trembling at that point. Terrified he'd be
disgusted by her, afraid to let her mind touch too closely on
what she might have caused. Trying to fight that memory.
That terrible memory of the blood, the hand, the lank of hair.

"This is not your fault, Violet."

She looked up at him, his great shoulders so easy to throw
her burdens upon.

"Whoever did this was reacting to a crime that Danvers
committed. Their reaction would have happened sooner or
later. What if he'd married Isolde and she'd been present?
Your actions might have saved your sister's life. We can't
know how things may have turned out." She nodded and then
said, "You'll need to talk to Fredericks."

Jack agreed.

"He'll talk more freely if I am there."

"Not Victor?"

She smiled and shook her head. "Fredericks was part of
Agatha's training. He spent time with all of us cousins that
Aunt Agatha raised. I didn't realize it at the time, but she
gave all of us the chance to learn to manage what she'd
created. I thought I might as well learn and apply to what
Victor and I had. It was why..." Violet stopped, overcome by
the death that mattered. It was why she'd been the one who
inherited. Of them all, she was the only one who'd listened
and learned.

"I understand," Jack said. "Bring Victor? Two o'clock?"

Violet agreed and Jack left. She didn't go back to the breakfast room but up to her bedroom. After a moment, she pulled out her journal and sent for tea.

The end of the morning passed with her admitting to herself as she wrote that her feelings for Jack would not be reasoned with, that she had no desire to go to Belgium, but she knew she'd be going all the same, and that she might have contributed to the situation that caused the death of a man.

A bad man, yes. But if history laid out the things that led to his death, her actions would be part of the reasons why. She had, however, acted in good faith in the attempt to save her sister from a man who had been a scoundrel. She could not let this result ruin her. All she could do, she realized, was trust that her good intentions mattered. That they both mattered and had consequences. Consequences both good and bad. Today her sister was still a free young girl, and a vile man had died.

Violet set her pen aside and made a list for Giles. She wanted another typewriter, and a journal for Isolde. She needed to learn the importance of discovering her thoughts and desires through writing. Perhaps, if journaling worked for Isolde as it did for both Violet and Victor, Isolde wouldn't be trapped by the plans of others again.

The last thing on the list was a book about Belgium. Violet didn't want to be unprepared for this trip. When that was done, she sent her request to Giles with Beatrice and then made a new list. On this one she put several names:

Helen Mathers
Harry Mathers
Markus Kennington
Norman Kennington
Mr. Gulliver

Mr. Higgins
Hugo Danvers

Unlike when she'd made a list of suspects after Aunt Agatha died, Violet didn't bother with putting Gerald or Victor's names on it. She didn't think even Jack believed that either of them were truly suspects. But she had to consider adding Father's. What if he'd learned that Danvers had been corrupting Helen Mathers? What if Father had learned that Isolde had been pressured into this wedding by the work of his wife and family? What if Father had learned that Danvers had intended to steal away Isolde and treat her poorly?

Would the same lion he'd imparted to Victor, Gerald, Peter, and Geoffrey appear? Violet had never seen that side of her father, but she'd seen it in her brothers often enough that she was certain it existed. Somewhere in his blood was the same conquering soul that had carved out a piece of England and a title for his heirs.

Slowly, she etched out the final name: Henry Carlyle.

CHAPTER TWELVE

Victor took Violet's coat as they entered the business offices. The man, Jones, was at his desk, ears red. He must have gotten quite a talking to at his reaction to Violet's earlier appearance. She grinned at him and said, "Blustery outside, isn't it?"

"Yes, m'lady. I..." The start of an apology appeared on his face.

Violet tut-tutted. "Think nothing of it."

His face turned even a more brilliant red, and Violet turned to see that Jack and Mr. Barnes had appeared behind them.

"Hullo," she said brightly. Jack searched her face carefully, so she pasted a happy smile on her face. It didn't reach her eyes, and she was sure he noticed. His mouth tightened, but neither of them said a thing. And neither of them pulled the wool over their companions' gazes. Victor and Mr. Barnes knew their counterparts far too well for that.

Mr. Fredericks already had a tea tray in the office and they all helped themselves before taking their seats.

"Lady Violet, how may I assist you?"

"You heard of Mr. Danvers's death?"

Fredericks nodded once, his face solemn and composed.

"I'm concerned that my actions regarding his investment scheme precipitated his death."

Fredericks frowned and adjusted the papers in front of him. He did not, however, provide her false comfort. He simply cleared his throat.

"It is possible, my lady. I have discovered rather a lot of money has been wrapped up in Mr. Danvers and those schemes."

Violet glanced at Jack and Mr. Barnes, who asked a series of questions about who had been involved.

"The small investors are unlikely to realize that there was a problem and to find it worth killing over," Barnes said. "Tell us the bigger names."

Fredericks glanced at Violet, who nodded, and he answered, "Mr. Markus Kennington, Mr. Norman Kennington, Lord Henry Carlyle." Fredericks paused and Victor shifted uncomfortably in his chair, but Violet had suspected their father's involvement might be the case before they'd appeared. Mr. Danvers had been too much in Lady Eleanor's pocket for it to be otherwise.

"Mr. Mathers?" Violet asked smoothly.

"He and Mr. Danvers had been partners for decades, m'lady. If anyone knew the true nature of what we suspect, it would be Mr. Mathers."

She wasn't surprised to hear Mr. Gulliver or Mr. Higgins involved when Fredericks continued. They'd worked with Danvers to try to corner Violet about her inheritance. She considered while the others murmured about guessed percentages and amounts. The details of the total amount invested was far less concerning than who had invested all they had. Violet was certain that Gerald wouldn't have done such a thing as invest everything, and he had the bulk of Father's money in his care.

She just couldn't put her father in the real suspect column. She had written his name on her list, but she didn't believe it. She might not *want* to believe it, but she was going to presume he wasn't the killer until she could no longer face anything else.

"Who," Violet asked, interrupting, "would lose everything should this investment scheme turn out to be what we suspect?"

Fredericks paused before speaking. "Certainly Higgins and Gulliver. Not your father or Mr. Markus Kennington. I have been unable to ascertain how much Mr. Norman Kennington invested. However, he does have some reliable incomes that would continue as long as he didn't mort-gage them to invest, and I do not believe that is the case."

Violet stood and started pacing Mr. Frederick's office. She noted it was dusted recently with the papers, except for the few in front of him, tucked into folders or drawers. She grinned and glanced at the men. Each of them was watching her pace.

Violet thought back to her list and wondered if people would kill if it wasn't all of their money.

"Where does Mr. Mathers get his income? Just with Danvers or did he have separate interests?"

"That isn't clear. He doesn't have debts racked about the city like Mr. Danvers. He paid his daughter's school bills on time. I can't be sure how much he might have lost."

Mr. Barnes finished with his questions. "This has been very helpful." He paused before asking, "Did Mr. Danvers intend to marry Isolde for her money?"

Mr. Fredericks said, "Lord Carlyle is very careful with his income and his children. The amount he invested was paltry compared to his wealth. What he set aside for Isolde is wrapped up tightly for her."

"Do you believe that Mr. Danvers was aware of that?"

"It is possible he was led to believe that he'd be able to access those funds upon their marriage."

Mr. Barnes's brows rose, and Victor answered the unspoken question. "Our stepmother. She has an infinite faith in her ability to sway my father with what he has to offer and how it will be laid out."

Violet finished. "We have a little half-brother, Geoffrey. He is the moon in her skies and the rest of us must fend for ourselves, and if she could give him everything, she would. He's also the youngest of us. Father will do his best for him, but Gerald and not bankrupting the estate is the priority."

Jack and Mr. Barnes gave their thanks and left, the official questioning over.

Violet asked Mr. Fredericks, "Was there anything you didn't share?"

Mr. Fredericks hesitated. "People have lost fortunes many times over, my lady. Any choices that were made because we prodded the house of cards doesn't mean responsibility lies at your feet. It would have all fallen apart eventually."

Violet agreed, and they discussed their own business for several minutes before Victor and Violet took their leave.

"Shall we lunch at that little Chinese food restaurant, darling?"

Violet thought that just the thing. They lingered over their dishes of noodles and chicken and their Chinese wine. They avoided going home, and Violet had to admit it was because she didn't want to hear Isolde chatter about Belgium. That made Violet think of Jack and made her second guess every little thing she'd said or done in the last few days, let alone when she'd been at Aunt Agatha's house and hadn't realized her infatuation would grow and grow.

She had journaled just that morning about the effect of him squatting down in front of her when she was at her end and how it made her feel. She couldn't deny it had been wonderful.

Delightful even. Delicate. Important. Important *to* someone.

She knew that she was important to Victor. She was discovering that she'd mattered to Isolde. Vi knew her father loved her in a distant sort of way and was realizing that despite the distance between her siblings caused by Lady Eleanor and being half-raised by Aunt Agatha, Vi's other siblings had loved and cared for her. She hadn't felt it until recently though. That realization mattered as did the realization that mattering to people changed her perspective about herself and her place in the world.

They had long since finished their meal when Violet asked suddenly, "What if we were to go visit Helen Mathers?"

"For condolences on the death of a lover who was throwing her over for someone with more money?" Victor's scoff was unwarranted in Violet's opinion, but she nodded. "You'll have to do better than that, love."

"As concerned friends," Violet suggested. "Who knew Helen attended the wedding and felt bad about..."

"We feel bad someone murdered someone else?" Victor smirked.

Vi scowled. "To...represent the family. A personal apology."

Victor drained his small wine glass and said, "It isn't like they can do much more than throw us out as we'll deserve. If you want to try it, I'm with you. Any idea where they live?"

Violet shook her head. "We can't ask Jack. He'd tell us to stay out of it. I wonder if Isolde knows where Helen lives."

Victor rang up their house and inquired, and they left the restaurant soon after with the address in hand. Victor left his car, and they took a cab simply because the driver had a far better chance of knowing how to get there.

The travel through London was slow, and Violet was bouncing as she pondered different ways to approach Helen. She finally determined on playing the concerned friend. It would very much be playacting as Violet and Helen only knew each other in passing, attending the same parties and whatnot before Violet had inherited and Helen had gotten caught up with her father's business partner. Violet shuddered. Being courted by Danvers would be very much like having poems read to the beauty of your eyes or other such nonsense—by your father.

This was *why* women had worked so hard to gain their rights. Of course, Violet supposed that those very rights gave Helen the choice to fall for her father's business partner. Just because Violet found it unwarrantable didn't mean she had to...oh! This was no time to be debating the rights of women. *How* could Violet get Helen to confide in her?

Perhaps just the weight of her silence? That was the method that Aunt Agatha used when Violet was a child. A leading question, a benign expression, a long silence. If you could wait out the intended victim, sometimes all you needed was the silence. Too often people couldn't stand the weight of it and filled it against their better interest.

The part of London where the Matherses lived didn't proclaim why someone like Danvers would seek them out. It wasn't over-the-top houses that shouted wealth and status. The house was, rather, a sturdy brick above with a garden, with a girl walking a dog in the park across the street from the houses, a woman feeding birds from a park bench, and a nanny letting children fly a kite and chase through the grass.

None of the houses were ostentatious, though they were all nice. None of them had stone lions, personalized gates, or topiary. Yet they were made of brick with cut lawns, clean streets, and the nice park available for their use.

This wasn't so very different from Victor's neighborhood actually. Violet examined each of the houses carefully and then they walked up to the door of number 18.

CHAPTER THIRTEEN

The door of Mather's house had been painted a deep garnet red and the knocker was a fanciful lion. Violet examined it before she used it and told Victor, "You should get one of those fun knockers, but a dragon instead."

"I don't have the same love for all things Asian as you do, luv. When Wakefield succeeds in binding you to him, you'll have to take a honeymoon and visit Japan or China. Hong Kong, perhaps? Buy one for yourself there and bring it back to your very English home."

Violet grinned at her brother. "I doubt very much that the British version of Asian things will be very much the same as they are there." She would have continued, but the door opened, revealing a middle-aged woman in a black dress.

"Hello," Violet said brightly. "Lord and Lady Carlyle for Helen Mathers. We're old friends."

"She's not here," the woman said with a tight mouth. It was nearly an accusation, as though Vi and Victor should know that Helen wasn't at home.

"Oh, that is too bad," Violet said. "We were so hoping to

have an outing with her and catch up on old times. Do you know when she'll return?"

"Won't be back for some time," the woman snapped.

"What about Mr. Mathers?" Victor inserted smoothly with the same bright smile. "We'd love to see him as well."

"They're both gone. Won't be back anytime soon. Leave your card if ya want."

Victor smoothly pulled a card out to leave with the woman, but before he did, he inquired again, "We saw her just recently."

"Gone sick, she has," the woman said. "Real sick. Don't think she'll be back for quite a while."

"Oh, I say," Victor said, keeping the genial tone but adding a touch of concern, "that is too bad. Is there somewhere we can send a get well chocolate or a card? Perhaps some flowers?"

The woman shook her head, took the card, and said, "I'll see she gets this." The door closed in their faces. The twins turned to each other and then glanced back at the door.

"What the devil?" Victor swore. "We just saw her. She was pale, I suppose. But so sick she had to leave home?"

Violet played with the ring on her finger as she thought over what she'd seen of Helen. She had been kissing Danvers rather fervently in that club. The action of a girl who'd been spurned? No. Perhaps, Vi thought, the action of a girl who hoped desperately that somehow the marriage would not come to pass. The act of a girl in love?

She'd seemed sick at the wedding. Maybe? Definitely sad. What if she had been in love? Or…Vi's brows rose as another, more terrible idea hit her. What if Helen had been expecting? What if Danvers had persuaded the girl into bed? She wasn't much older than Isolde. Would she know how to protect herself against an unwanted result?

What would a girl like Helen do if she found herself in

such a condition and the man who had been the father had intended to marry another? That would leave one heart-broken and listless. Pale and sick looking. It was all conjecture, of course, but possible.

She placed her hand on Victor's arm, knowing he'd never had to think of such things, and they started down the path to their car. The girl with the large spaniel from the park stood there, hand on the leash of her dog.

"Hullo, there," Victor said charmingly. He could be quite persuasive to the opposite sex, and Violet watched him almost angrily as he introduced them and asked, "The younger Miss Mathers?"

The girl nodded. Her dimple was flashing and she gazed up at Victor with a wide, shocked gaze when he turned his attention to her.

"Whatever are you doing here instead of school?" Vi's tone wasn't accusatory.

"Oh...I came home to spend the weekend with the family and...something came up."

"We heard your sister was quite ill," Violet said. "We're so concerned."

Something in the girl's face said that at least part of what they'd heard was a lie. Victor started to inquire, but Vi squeezed his elbow and he glanced at her. She shook her head slightly, and they turned inquiring gazes at the girl.

"What is your name?"

"Anna." The girl dimpled again and cast another look at Victor.

"Would it be all right, do you think? If we were to take you for an ice cream?"

The girl glanced at the house, at the twins, and the promise of sweets seemed to be enough to get her to take the dog inside and slip back out.

Victor seated Anna in the car as though he were escorting her personally while Violet placed herself in the back seat.

"Are you quite close to Helen?"

The girl hesitated before answering. "We used to be quite close. When we were both at school. Now..."

"It's hard when you get separated, isn't it? Victor and I were, of course, since he went to the boys' school and I to the girls'. Even in the same town, it was hard to see each other."

Victor glanced at Vi. "We used to sneak out at night and meet. Run wild. Got sent down from school a few times for that."

"And we had a drop place where we'd leave each other notes and things. Ciphers for a while when we were obsessed with spy novels." Violet grinned and winked as Victor parked the automobile.

They all ordered ice cream and found a little table to enjoy the treat.

"Tell us about Helen," Violet said, nudging her brother. "What happened? How can we help?"

The girl glanced between them and then down at her ice cream. Her face went solemn and worried, and Violet asked, "Is it her lover?"

The girl glanced up at Vi with a swift expression and then at Victor before returning to playing with her ice cream.

"Victor," Violet said, "would you be so good as to go get me some more paper from that little shop while we're here? And maybe some things for Anna to take back to school with her. Are you going soon?"

"Tomorrow," she said, her mouth squirming up into a scowl.

Victor nodded and rose.

"Buy for her," Violet said before he stepped away, "like her sister would. Sisters spoil each other, you know."

As soon as Victor was gone, Violet reached out and took

Anna's hand. "I know about having a little sister. Sometimes we need our big sisters and don't have them. Talk me to me as though I were Helen, and I'll do my best for you."

The girl bit her lip and Violet waited. She had to admire the tenacity of the girl. She fought telling all, but the silence and her worries were too much for her.

"She...it was the lover. She...she...he was going to marry someone else. Someone he didn't love. For the money!"

Violet gasped appropriately and kept her gentle hand on Anna's. She squeezed it lightly.

"Poor Helen."

"He was never good enough for her!"

"They never are," Violet agreed gently.

"It was worse than that. He was rich and she wanted to be rich. Always flashing about money. Papa works hard for us. He puts money aside, watches every little purchase. But he's quite strict with purchases and allowances. Helen hated it. All our friends have spending money, buckets of it. But we barely have enough for things we actually need."

Violet could imagine how hard that would be, especially at a school for wealthy girls without the corresponding allowance. Helen must have been slighted and teased often.

"She always swore she'd find a rich man someday. One who would spoil her. And when she found one, he was...well...he wasn't what you'd want."

"Older?" Violet asked.

Anna nodded and whispered, "Older even than Papa. And fat!"

"Oh," Violet moaned. "Helen is so beautiful. She could have someone else."

"But she didn't want to wait," Anna said. "She didn't like being home from school and not having any money. Papa keeps an eye on where she goes, too. But he trusted this man, so he'd let *him* take her out and not the men more her age."

"Oh, your poor sister. I feel quite angry for her."

Anna nodded, not seeing the gleam in Vi's eye. She *did* feel quite sorry for Helen, but any girl who decided that Danvers was the best bet had to be sick in the head.

"So she...well...I shouldn't say."

"Talk to me like I'm your sister," Violet instructed. "You need to get this off your chest before you go back to school or it'll wear you down and you'll find yourself telling some untrustworthy young miss."

Anna looked alarmed at that idea and when Violet waited yet again, Anna finally continued. "Helen thought that she had to let him...well...you know..."

Violet nodded.

"And then she found out..."

"There was a result," Violet said gently.

Anna nodded, glancing around to ensure no one was listening and then she hissed, "But then he threw her over for a richer girl. Papa said it was better, the man was too old for Helen.

She should have never imagined that it would be anything other than him showing Helen about.

Papa didn't realize that they'd...well...and that Helen was...well..."

Violet nodded. It was as she suspected. She didn't need Anna to say the words aloud.

"Did she try to end it?"

Anna shook her head. "She couldn't find anywhere. She doesn't know anyone who would know how. Helen wasn't feeling well. Being alone without getting out was too hard. She's quite needy to interact with others. She gets blue when she doesn't. All of that together, she was just... sad." The look at Anna's face told Vi the depth of that sadness. It had been too much for the poor, spurned girl.

Violet leaned back, shocked. "I see..."

Helen had tried to end herself, not the baby. Violet wanted to murder Danvers herself. He'd ruined the heart of a young girl and had expected her to arrive at the wedding. Of all the dastardly, no good, *evil* things to do to a poor girl barely out of the schoolroom. And to imagine him flailing about on the top of poor—Violet shuddered and put the idea out of her head before she sicked-up in her bowl of melted ice cream.

"Listen to me," Violet said gently. "Your sister is sad. I hope your father is taking her somewhere that will see to her."

"I threw a fit until he swore he'd take her to the seaside. She feels better in the sun. I made him swear he'd be kind. He was so angry. I'd never seen him like that. But he wasn't angry at her. He was sad for her. So, I think...I think..."

"The sun will be just the thing. The sun, time, healing. It just takes time. You write to your sister. Remind her of good things. Send her books and letters and things to keep her mind filled. Make your father use that money he has put away." Violet pulled out a notebook from her drawstring bag. "Give me your address at school."

Anna listed it off.

"And Helen's address."

Anna hesitated and then listed it off.

Violet said, "I will send her a care package as you have never seen before."

Anna grinned and squealed a little.

Violet frowned, thoughtful, then told Anna, "I will be your patroness. Expect a small allowance from me."

The girl's mouth dropped.

"You are bright. You are kind. You are loving. In return, you swear to me you will do well in school. It's a new day for women, but only if we take it. Will you take it?"

The girl nodded.

"You'll work hard?"

She nodded, eyes wide.

"Qualify for college, and I'll see to it you can go. Now, put Helen out of your mind beyond your letters and care. Your sister will get better. Things will improve with time. She has escaped that fiend even if she doesn't know it yet. She will realize it one day."

Anna nodded, and as she finished her ice cream, Violet made a list of things that Hargreaves would need to see regularly sent to the girl with her allowance. If Violet was going to be in Belgium with Isolde, preventing sadness and being locked away from turning her into Helen, then someone else would need to see to the day-to-day of caring for the girl.

"Thank you, love," Violet told her as they walked back out to the car and found Victor with a large box. "I will be careful with your confidences. I look forward to our alliance." Violet turned to her brother. "Victor, give her your card. I expect to hear how you are doing at school," she said to Anna. "And a report of when you'll be back in London, so we can get together and have a good gossip. Send me the details of all your friends, so I'm ready to discuss the ins and outs."

Anna nodded, and they returned her home chattering brightly. The shadows were gone from her eyes when they reached the house, and she squealed as Victor walked her up to the house with the large box and saw her inside.

When he returned to the car, he said, "I don't know what you said to her, but whatever it was—it was well done."

"I'll be giving her the first of scholarships for girls in Aunt Agatha's name. If her father was clever with how he moved money, Anna might get out of this mess with something to support her. But if he was not, she might lose everything. I won't have her lose schooling and the life that was promised."

"It was a stolen life," Victor said.

"She didn't steal it, though, did she? She's a good kid. I feel certain Aunt Agatha would approve."

"Then my approval means nothing next to that." He grinned, but he took her hand and squeezed and the approval in his eyes meant everything.

"Not true, brother." She winked. "Just less."

"And where does Jack fall in the line-up?" An elbow in Victor's side was his answer.

CHAPTER FOURTEEN

They walked into the house and saw Hargreaves hovering anxiously outside of the parlor. The twins glanced at each other.

"Uh oh. I'll endeavor to see what is wrong." Violet handed Hargreaves her coat and walked into the parlor. Her gaze narrowed on the sight before her. Her sister was sitting on a settee and Hugo Danvers had pressed far too close.

As she entered, she could hear him murmur, "Do you remember when we first met?"

Violet watched the two of them, who had yet to notice her presence. Isolde shook her head and leaned back. Hugo leaned closer.

"I remember it like it was yesterday," he murmured. He was speaking like a lover and his tone made Vi ill. As far as Hugo Danvers knew, Isolde had lost her intended and was in mourning. "Your hair was flowing down your back, you wore this pale pink dress. You looked like an angel. I've always thought of you as an angel."

"I..." Isolde scooted over a little as Hugo took her hand.

"I know that you were pressured into the alliance with my father." Hugo said 'father' like it was a curse. "I'll make sure that never happens again."

Vi's gaze narrowed on him. Who was he to protect Isolde? No one!

"I..." Isolde's head was turned so that she could still see Hugo but arched as far away from him as she could be. The angle of her neck had to be painful, but Hugo didn't seem to notice. Or, perhaps, he did not care. "Please..."

Hugo didn't listen to her pleading. Violet noted the way Isolde was tugging her hand away from Hugo, but he didn't seem to notice. There were fingerprints on Isolde's skin where he was digging in.

"Our condolences on the loss of your father," Violet told Hugo, announcing her presence.

They both started. Isolde's expression flashed with relief while Hugo looked as though Violet was very unwelcome. He had yet to learn her capacity for making him unwelcome.

She crossed and took Isolde's hand, pulling her to her feet. Hugo's expression was utterly shocked as Violet forced him to scoot back and wrapped her arm around her sister. Vi seated Isolde next to herself on the Chesterfield, with Isolde tucked between her and the side of the sofa.

"I imagine," Violet continued, as though she hadn't just pulled that maneuver, "that your father's death was quite the shock."

"It was, of course. Thank you," Hugo replied.

The expression on his face declared he'd like to see the last of Violet. It wasn't Violet, however, that he'd be seeing the last of. He waited and as he did Victor entered the room, took in Violet's position, the way Isolde was cowering behind her elder sister, and his eyes narrowed. "What are you doing here?" Victor demanded.

Hugo cleared his throat and adjusted his awkward seat to state, "Just giving Isolde my condolences."

"Which you've done," Victor said. The indication was clear that Hugo was invited to leave.

Hugo's head cocked, and he looked quizzical.

Violet could feel Isolde shuddering under her hand. Vi's furious face told Victor all he needed to know.

"Have I done something to offend you?" Hugo asked, refusing to stand. "Surely, as Isolde and I have experienced the greatest loss, it is reasonable that we are best able to comfort each other."

"Is that the lie you are telling yourself?" Victor wasn't even pretending at manners. "You think it is acceptable to visit a very young, very shocked girl at home alone? After such a harrowing trial?"

"Besides," Violet said lightly, "you said yourself you knew that Isolde was pressured into a relationship with your father. You know she isn't grieving as you must be, so why did you come?"

Hugo glanced between the twins and then seemed to appeal to Isolde, but Violet did her best to block his view of her little sister.

"Leave, Danvers," Victor said. "It's long past time for you to go."

"You can't keep me from Isolde. This isn't a prison."

Isolde squeaked, and as they all turned to look at her, she tucked her face into Violet's shoulder.

Violet lifted a single brow at Hugo and his face flushed furiously.

"This isn't quite the thing, and you are well aware your behavior isn't apropos. Did you wait until we'd left her alone or did you inquire to see if she was alone when you appeared?"

Hugo flushed and didn't answer.

Victor continued. "Once this murder investigation is over, Isolde will be leaving London and you will not see her again."

Hugo almost growled, and Isolde shuddered at the noise.

"Now I say—" Hugo tried.

"Out," Victor demanded, interrupting him.

"Isolde is nearly family," Hugo protested.

"Isolde," Violet said, "is with her family. And the only other connections she'll be forming is with other travelers and then college students."

"College?"

"College," Victor repeated. "Not another *too old* for her beau who wishes to pressure her into something she doesn't want."

Hugo was brilliantly red at that point, but he turned and appealed to Isolde. "You wish to *leave*? Leave? Travel? College?"

Violet would have answered for her sister, but he needed to hear it from Isolde, and she needed to learn how to speak for herself. Seeing her as crumpled as she'd been when Vi had arrived had shown just how easy it was to squash the burgeoning independent woman in Isolde.

Violet nudged Isolde, and she said, "I...I...do."

"You don't have to do that," Hugo declared. "You have *options*."

When Isolde didn't speak, Vi nudged her again, and Isolde said, "I *want* to go to college.

And to travel. And to breathe a little after...everything."

Victor stepped forward. He was shorter and more slender than Hugo, but Victor still seemed intimidating.

"You heard it from her. You heard it from me. Out. Don't bother her again."

Hugo snarled as he slammed from the parlor. Victor followed.

Isolde moaned as he left, curling onto her side and placing her head on Violet's lap. "Oh, that was awful!"

Violet ran her hand along her sister's back, soothing her as Vi would a baby. Over and over again until Isolde was quivering, and then finally, she started to cry. She didn't talk as she cried, just let the tears fall slowly and silently.

Violet didn't say a word either. Isolde needed to have a good cry. Not just over Danvers dying, though perhaps also that, but over the fact that her mother had cornered her into a marriage that was clearly destined for misery.

Victor returned long enough to see Isolde weeping and left in a fury. After quite a long while, Isolde slipped into sleep. Violet left her and found that Jack had arrived again.

"I was hoping to ask a few questions of Isolde, only..."

Violet shook her head. "Maybe we can help? She barely fell asleep, and given the circles under her eyes I don't think she's been sleeping well—perhaps for weeks." Victor snorted. "Jack is here because he knows Cook is excellent."

"It's hours before dinner," Jack protested.

"And just in time for tea," Violet said with a grin and a wink. "Hargreaves, in the library, please. Leave Isolde be and let her sleep."

"Yes, m'lady," he said.

Beatrice brought in the tea, which was cucumber or smoked salmon sandwiches, scones with clotted cream and jam, and fruit tarts. Jack asked about the Kenningtons, and they had to admit they didn't know much regarding the details of those connections.

"We've been pursuing a few leads that have been harder to track down than I'd have expected."

"Perhaps," Violet suggested as she set down her cucumber sandwich, "you are referring to Mr. Mathers and his daughter?"

Jack's gaze narrowed on her, and she knew that she'd given away they'd inquired into the murder.

"We might have stopped by to see Helen," Violet admitted.

"Perhaps. Maybe. If you aren't too angry," Victor mocked.

Violet nudged him with her elbow and confessed, "It is possible that in stopping by we took Helen's little sister out for ice cream, and she and I gossiped a bit."

Jack frowned. She could almost see him debating. He wanted to know what she'd discovered and he wanted to scold her thoroughly. She waited to see what he'd choose.

He finally said, "We wouldn't have gotten anywhere with that angle."

Violet grinned at him and Victor clapped Jack on the back. "Bravo, good man! Way to accept the inevitable."

Jack scowled at them. Vi ignored his expression. "Anna revealed that Helen attempted to take her own life."

Jack started and Victor's smile slipped away. Nothing about that was humorous.

"It seems that she pursued Mr. Danvers and thought they would be married. After he led her to the conclusion that they would marry, he was able to persuade her to physical relations and left her with a little burden. Only after did he throw Helen over for Isolde."

Jack set down his teacup.

"Anna told me that her father took Helen to the seaside. It sounds like she's prone towards fits of being blue and this pushed her past her capacity. Her father took her to Margate to recover. The address is in my book."

"I'll be needing that," Jack stated. "We know, of course, that Mathers is Danvers's partner. The level of Mathers's illegal machinations is unclear. I suspect that Mathers knew exactly what was happening but kept everything he did monetarily hidden. He was very, very careful. One of the numbers boys over at the Yard said that he didn't think Mathers would be ruined when Danvers's scheme eventually fell apart. The fellow said he thought Danvers must have intended to take what he could and run just before it all fell apart. There was no sustaining this scheme."

Violet passed around a tray of sandwiches while Jack continued. "We spoke with everyone who invested. No one has any idea that their investment was a sham and that Mathers was anything other than a minion for Danvers."

Violet sipped her tea and considered. She didn't love that Mr. Mathers had assisted in stealing money for a sham investment scheme, but she was glad that the girls would survive.

"He seems to be a real pull-himself-up-by-his-bootstraps type," Jack said. "Built a fortune out of nothing. He's a widower, never remarried. Goes to church. The churchgoers like him. He volunteers. Gives money. Goes to all the school things for his daughters that he can.

There is no indication he's involved in criminal activity by any of the rest of his activities."

Violet refilled the teacups for them. "Perhaps he feels guilty for his life."

"Perhaps," Victor said doubtfully. "Surely you'd just stop. If you're smart enough to get involved in this stuff and to keep it from coming back at you, you're smart enough to work a job that doesn't include stealing."

Jack nodded. Both he and Victor reached for more sandwiches while Violet debated the idea of Mathers.

Was it possible to be both a good community man and a thief? She didn't see how. She tucked a lock of hair behind her ear and played with the ring on her finger while the two men started debating cricket and stopped talking about the crime.

Violet avoided the scolding she knew Jack intended when Isolde woke and asked for her sister. Vi left with a wink towards Victor, who just might get that scolding instead.

By the time that Isolde had bathed, been put to bed with a sleeping pill, and talked to about Belgium until she succumbed to sleep, Jack had gone.

"Should we go out?" Victor asked.

Vi shook her head. "Is it too awful of me if I want to stay in and write?"

Victor laughed. "We got lazy and weak in Italy, darling. We'll have to build up our capacity to those old days of late nights and drinks with the pals."

They discussed the plot of their story, ate a bowl of warm soup, and agreed that they'd be scolded from one year to the next if they didn't soon inquire after Father and Lady Eleanor.

Violet thought the only reason the earl and his lady hadn't descended on the errant children yet was because Gerald had most likely sent the appropriate messages—ones that they hadn't been wise enough to do themselves.

CHAPTER FIFTEEN

In the morning, Victor and Violet ate together. Vi had stopped by Isolde's room long enough to tell her to spend the day lazing in bed, looking at magazines, and that she was not to have any callers. It would have been the type of thing a controlling guardian said if Isolde didn't know it was to keep Hugo Danvers away.

"The servants have also been informed that you are not at home to anyone except Gerald."

"I haven't stayed in bed and lolled about before. Not unless I was sick."

"You are sick, dear," Violet told her, "or at least that is what we're telling your mother and Father."

Violet turned to leave when Isolde asked, "Why don't you call her Mother?"

Vi thought about lying to her sister, but the time for softening truth for Isolde was past, and it was time for her to learn. "She never was. Not to Victor and me. Aunt Agatha demanded us and Lady Eleanor was happy to see us off and out of the way."

"Oh," Isolde said, suddenly seeing their lifetime anew.

Violet smiled gently. "I'll check in when we get home."

The drive out to Kennington house started the moment they'd finished breakfast and downed enough coffee to see them through the drive. They had Giles drive and chatted about Isolde and Jack on the way.

"Are you in love?" Victor asked, as Violet mentioned the investigation and how clever Jack was at discovering the details of someone's life.

Violet played with the ring on her finger and admitted, "I...might be on the journey, but I'm not there yet."

"The journey?" Victor laughed. "You're head over heels, little love. Jack might be worse.

I think he swallowed his tongue yesterday to keep from letting you have it after your stunt with

Anna. If it had been anyone else, they'd have gotten their ears boxed."

Violet sniffed and played with her ring again. "Did you want to go to the club tonight?" Victor agreed, and they both took a deep breath as Giles parked the car in front of Kennington House.

As they approached the house, Violet asked, "United?"

"Always."

Morton opened the door and they asked for their father. The earl's property was in the south of England, so they hadn't left Kennington House yet to take the journey home. Their father did have a house in London, but Vi imagined that having your future son-in-law murdered just before the wedding made a little distance from town more desirable than access to his clubs and restaurants.

They were led into a parlor with furniture that may have been purchased new just after Waterloo. It felt old and rich but a little shabby. Violet picked up a small box and realized it was encrusted in real jewels and just sitting out in a nearly unused room. The Kenningtons were quite wealthy, Vi thought. Wealthy enough to not worry so much about their investment? No one wanted to be stolen from, but was it a crime so dastardly to drive someone who kept priceless boxes sitting out?

Father arrived almost immediately.

"Your mother has taken to her bed," he said.

Violet prevented an expression from betraying her thoughts as she kissed his cheek. "Isolde isn't feeling well either. She wanted us to bring her love. Father, Victor and I would like permission to take her on a trip as soon as the murderer is caught."

He nodded his assent, and they all took a seat, staring at each other as he said, "Where will you go then?"

"Isolde has a desire to see Bruges," Victor said. "Vi and I haven't been there. You know Vi, she's already got a book about it and histories of travels to that land as though it were Lilliput. Vi has Isolde making a list of things she wants to see and hikes she wants to take. Or whatever it is that people do there."

Father grunted. "Thinking of leaving Eleanor here. She won't get out of bed and to be honest, I prefer rather less time around this brother and cousin of hers. Maybe I'll come with you. Haven't been to Belgium since I went on my Grand Tour. M'father sent me with a cousin of his. Might be good for us both to get away."

"Father," Violet said carefully, "it does seem that, perhaps, Isolde wasn't aware of your concerns between herself and Danvers."

Father looked startled. "I talked to her mother about it."

Violet and Victor glanced at each other but said nothing.

Their father's expression went from quizzical to understanding and a rare flash of anger passed over his face.

"Ah, well." Father cleared his throat as he regained control. "Ring the bell, little one.

Let's have some tea."

Earl grey, custard buttons, and a little almond gingerbread, which they mostly just nibbled at, later, and Father said, "Yes. Take her to Belgium or wherever else she wants to go.

Does she know what she wants after this trip of yours?"

"I think it would be good for her to go to college. Perhaps spend a little time spreading her wings before another marriage could be considered," Violet said idly, putting another slice of gingerbread on her father's plate and refilling his tea.

He grunted. "I'll have my man see about getting her into college."

The awkward silence after that statement was filled with Violet discussing the weather and Victor the outcome of a recent horse race.

Finally, Violet decided to set aside the manners that had been ground into her and asked, "Father, if Danvers's investment scheme is a sham, will Markus or Norman Kennington lose their shirts?"

Father started and the scolding look he gave her would have shriveled her if there hadn't been a murder on the line.

"Father," Victor said, "were you aware that Violet reasoned out who killed Aunt Agatha?"

Father harrumphed. "Course I did. Now you think it was one of the Kennington men that did in Danvers?"

Violet carefully licked her lips and admitted, "Papa, it seems certain that the investment scheme was just that. Those who put their money in won't be getting it back."

His brows rose at that. "Invested m'self. Heard from Markus that it was a sure thing.

Must be what they've been having a fizz about."

"Has there been a ruckus here?"

Father nodded. "Likely why Markus and Norman or their wives haven't appeared. Those wives of theirs have been in bed nearly as much as Eleanor. Was thinking that they were making a big thing out of our scandal. Seems they have their own crosses to bear." He hummed under his breath and said, "Think I'll take your mother to Paris. Good time to be traveling for all of us.

Can't imagine you'd want these old ones about."

"Father, the trip to America on those steamships is said to be quite agreeable. Victor and I have heard it from a few friends. New York City has got much to offer, and I was just reading an article about Cuba. You might like that too."

Father harrumphed again. "You getting involved in this case, too?"

Violet and Victor glanced at each other.

"It is an interesting puzzle, isn't it?" Victor mused. "Who realized their money was gone forever? Who felt it was worth killing over? Perhaps Danvers was the engineer of some other crime we know nothing of."

Father took the last piece of gingerbread and ate half of it in one bite before speaking. "I can't imagine it was Markus or Donald."

"Because you've known them so long?"

Father shook his head. "They might have invested all of their ready money, but they have even more money wrapped up tight. Income from their estates. They, both of them, might have been hard hit. But enough to murder Danvers? Besides, Norman has a blood problem."

"Problem?" Violet asked and smiled as her father smirked for a moment.

"Can't abide the sight of it. Makes him quite sick. Seen him go down myself. Like a tree.

One moment standing. Next flat out on the ground."

Victor chuckled, but Violet couldn't help but remember

what she'd seen. The pool of blood. The flop of glued together hair. The lifeless hand. The...don't think of it, she told herself, and somehow her thoughts conveyed the command in Jack's voice.

"Changes the whole perspective, doesn't it?" her father continued. "I heard from your mother that you've been seeing a Scotland Yard fellow. Was it one of the ones who came here?"

"Yes sir. I met Jack Wakefield at Aunt Agatha's." Vi's heart was in her throat as she waited for Father's opinion.

"James Wakefield is a friend of mine. Not like Markus, of course. Wakefield's a good man. His son seems quite sharp."

"He was in the military police," Victor told Father. "He doesn't *have* to work, of course, but the Yard calls Jack in here and there when there's a case that seems appropriate to his skills."

"Probably our types," Father replied. He sniffed and said, "Rich, titled, gentry folks. You come with questions and an Oxford education, connections to your family, memberships at the same club. Ain't so easy to lean back on your laurels, then, is it?"

Violet was breathing a little easier as she realized her father didn't object. She took in a bit of a shuddering breath and elbowed Victor when he smirked. Father caught the byplay and smiled at the two of them.

"You two always were the same. Troublesome from day one. Squalling for weeks and weeks. Once you could walk... madness. As soon as you could open doors, well, we lost more than one nanny, I'll tell you. Your mother, Belinda, she used to laugh and laugh. Said you spoke on another level. Loved everything about that."

Father looked sorrowful. "Neither one of you spoke for a few weeks after we lost her. You didn't start talking until Agatha came. She scooped you up. Took you for a ride in her carriage. When you came back, you weren't better. Not for a while yet. But you answered when you were asked if you wanted a biscuit. Never could thank her enough after that."

Victor wrapped his arm around Violet, whose vision had gone blurry with the story of her mother.

"I wish I could have known her," Vi admitted.

"You're very like her," Father said and then abruptly rose. "Think I'll go tell my man to pack my things. Need to be careful, Vi, if you're going to nose about in this business. Can't imagine whoever the murderer is would take kindly to you sticking your oar in."

Father left, and Victor and Violet waited. Should they further stick their oar in, as Father put it?

"We came all this way," Victor said, knowing her thoughts, "so we might as well go ahead and talk to Markus. He must be around, mustn't he?"

Violet wasn't sure, but they rang the bell to have the tea things taken away and inquired after the homeowner. He was in his office, and they brazenly knocked on his door and entered before he could turn them away.

"Didn't expect to see you two," he said, carefully closing the file on his desk and gesturing to the chairs in front of his desk. "What it's all about?"

"Been discussing recent events." Victor took a seat. "Were you aware Danvers tried to force his way into our finances? He attempted to tell our man of business that we had said to join in the scheme."

Kennington's brows rose and two small circles of red appeared on his cheeks, but he said nothing.

Violet smiled brightly and reminded herself that they all assumed she was an idiot, being both younger and female. "Mr. Fredericks, isn't he just brilliant, Vic?"

Victor gave her a side-eyed mocking look but agreed. "He is quite brilliant. Refused point-blank to invest without our express permission. Then, he looked into matters as he might have if we'd asked him about it."

"What does this have to do with me?"

"Well, you invested, didn't you?" Victor said smoothly, with an arched brow. "You invested, and you allowed Danvers to become engaged to your niece despite the clear imbalance of the situation. You and Lady Eleanor bought the whole charade."

The two circles of red had slowly spread across Markus's cheeks and his gaze narrowed threateningly on Victor.

"Then you attacked him with Gulliver outside of the house on the wedding day. Was that when you realized it was all a sham?"

"Are you the blighters who set the Yard on me?" Kennington demanded. "With these starts at hares? Faradiddles and nonsense!"

"It's hardly starting at a hare to know that someone invested money in a fraudulent scheme and was seen assaulting the victim." Victor's voice was smooth and even, but very imperious. It was clear who was the earl's son and who was not.

Violet crossed her ankles and told herself to leave it to Victor. With Markus, she would get nowhere.

"Were you also aware of his lover? Did you know that he made her promises and left her with a growing bundle?"

The way fury rolled down Kennington's neck, turning his ears to a brilliant red, told Violet that he was aware of Helen's existence at the least. Violet hadn't had feelings towards him one way or the other before this, but she would never respect him again.

"I knew that things had gone farther between the chit and Danvers than most knew.

Farther than Mathers knew. Who do you really think had cause to kill him? Me? I'm not ruined. Or that girl's father and long-time friend? Get out of here. Take your accusations with you and don't come back until I have abject apologies from the both of you."

Violet rose and pulled Victor up with her. Anything he said to them wouldn't be reliable. Just as Victor reached to open the door, Markus said, "Your father invested. Gulliver.

Higgins. Not just me. Don't forget that son of his. Hugo hated his father as much as you two hate Eleanor."

Violet turned at that. "I don't hate Eleanor. Neither of us do."

Markus's scoff-filled laugh told her what he thought of the statement. She wouldn't defend it to him. Not any more than he'd defend himself to her. They were done here.

CHAPTER SIXTEEN

"We came all this way," Violet said. "You see if Norman is still here and if you cut yourself in his presence, see if he really faints. I'm going to face the dragon."

Victor winced for Violet, who took a deep breath and then hurried up the stairs to her stepmother's room. It was the same room she'd had before she'd married. The wall outside the door showed Eleanor as she had been then, with her blue eyes, golden hair and figure that hadn't been marred by carrying two children. Her lips were pink, and she was smiling at something that only she could see.

She looked lovely. Not just on the exterior, but on the interior. Violet wished she'd known this version of her stepmother rather than the one who had always seen Vi and Victor as competition for her own offspring. Surely Father had love enough for them all? But Eleanor had always been jealous of whatever affection Father had had for the twins, She was the type to *do her duty* when it came to the twins, but she was quick to push them to school and their holidays with Aunt Agatha.

Violet tapped on the door of her stepmother's room and reminded herself of all the good things. She had tried to encourage them into security. She truly did feel that marriage was the best choice for a woman and had never tried to push Violet into the mess that had landed Isolde.

Why had Eleanor let it come to that with Isolde?

"Yes?"

Violet opened the door enough to stick her head in. "Hullo there, I was hoping you felt well enough for me to stop in?"

Eleanor scowled at Violet. "I suppose you've come to gloat? You were right about Carlton. I was wrong."

It took Violet a moment to remember that Carlton was Danvers's first name.

"No, of course not," Violet told her gently, keeping the good memories at the forefront of her mind. "I've always known that you saw marriage as the best for Isolde and myself. Mr. Danvers presented security for her."

Lady Eleanor sniffled into a lace handkerchief. "He did. I was just doing my best. How was I supposed to know he was a bounder?"

Violet refrained from pointing out that she'd also disregarded the objections of her husband, her eldest stepson, and her daughter all to see Isolde married to a man who seemed to be wealthy. Money before all else.

"Father has decided that Isolde would do well to keep close to Victor's house and then spend some time overseas. We've selected Bruges since it will be an out-of-the-way place to let things die down."

Lady Eleanor sniffled again. "Will you be bringing any of your friends? Isn't Victor quite good friends with that St. Marks heir? He might do well for Isolde."

Violet turned to close the door and hide her expression.

Firstly, Tomas was in love with Violet. Secondly, he was still recovering from the horrors of the war. Thirdly, he was astoundingly wealthy. All Lady Eleanor would care about was, of course, the wealth. At least he was only a couple years older than the twins rather than decades older than Isolde.

Violet smiled a reply since she couldn't think of anything to say that wouldn't set off her stepmother. Vi seated herself in the chair next to the bed, noted the teapot and refilled a cup for her stepmother, then rang the bell for a fresh pot.

By the time she escaped Kennington House, she'd be swimming in tea, but Lady Eleanor was always more likely to gossip over tea. Violet thought it might just be muscle memory since many a morning, Lady Eleanor was usually doing just that with her friends.

Vi ordered tea from the maid who arrived.

"You do look peaked, Lady Eleanor," Violet said. "Perhaps Victor and I can hunt up some favorite chocolates? Those would cheer you, wouldn't they?"

Lady Eleanor softened at the idea of it and mentioned a few favorites. "Is my Isolde recovering well? The poor thing. To lose her betrothed on her wedding day!"

Ah, Violet thought, they were going to ignore the decision to call off the wedding. For the best, perhaps, given the results of the day.

"She is quite upset," Violet said. "She had to take a sleeping pill to rest after she had a good cry yesterday."

"She must be asking for me," Lady Eleanor said, and Violet nodded fervently.

"Nothing helps like the touch and care of a mother," Vi agreed, "but she knows Papa wants her out of the house, away from the scene, and tucked up tight. Victor's house is quite nice, you know. Large and well-appointed."

Lady Eleanor let Vi change the subject to the number of

rooms, the size of the garden, the likelihood of rain. When Lady Eleanor seemed in quite a good mood, Violet asked, "Did Hugo Danvers bother Isolde before?"

Lady Eleanor frowned at the question. "Why would he?"

"He came by to see how Isolde was doing," Violet told her.

"Quite properly," Lady Eleanor stated firmly.

"He seemed to be...enchanted by her."

Lady Eleanor's instinctive reaction to assume Violet was incorrect seemed to fight with her desire to have her daughter acknowledged as the most lovely and enchanting of young ladies.

Finally, she said, "He did seem to spend quite a lot of time with his father and Carlton's friends. You know, he didn't work with his father. I always thought that was odd. Here was Carlton with his successful business and Hugo insisted on going his own way."

Violet took a sip of her tea and made sure to cock her head inquisitively as Lady Eleanor brought up the sons who took after their fathers and worked the family business and estates. She seemed to have adjusted the past to ignore the fact that Danvers had been a fraud.

Violet let Lady Eleanor carry on about one of her friend's sons who insisted on pursuing the church even though such a course was no longer in fashion.

"It isn't 1804, now is it?" Lady Eleanor laughed into her handkerchief at the expense of the homely Cecil Brown, who had returned from the war changed.

Violet's thoughts regarding everything Lady Eleanor had said wouldn't have helped the situation, so she listened without a word.

When Lady Eleanor paused, Violet asked, "Did you know Helen Mathers?"

"The daughter of the assistant?" Lady Eleanor's hands

pressed together tightly, fingers digging into her flesh, and Violet could see her stepmother had known exactly who Helen had been to Danvers.

Violet didn't press further on their relationship and simply said, "I understand she's fallen ill. Her father has taken her out of town."

"The girl needs to be reined in. Hopefully, he will see to it. Wild. This is what comes of letting young ladies think they're as capable as young men."

Violet snapped her mouth shut and refilled Lady Eleanor's cup before fluffing the pillows behind her. "What does Hugo Danvers do for a living?" Violet asked.

"I don't know, actually," Lady Eleanor said. "Carlton and Hugo spent enough time together, but there didn't seem to be love lost between them. Perhaps Hugo just lived off of his father. They were sneaky about the way they felt. You had to be paying attention. Isolde..." Lady Eleanor's comment cut off, and Violet suddenly wondered if her stepmother knew that Hugo had feelings for Isolde.

Had Vi's sister turned to her mother for help in dealing with Hugo? If so...then Lady Eleanor had failed again.

"I don't care for him," Vi said.

"You have been remarkably pleasant this afternoon, Vi. But I think I will nap. Your father states we must leave tomorrow and I must gather my strength."

"Of course." Violet pressed her stepmother's hand and rose to go.

"Just a word to the wise, dear," Lady Eleanor said, stopping Violet before she was more than a step or two from the bed. "Your father has heard of the flirtation between yourself and the Scotland Yard detective."

Violet's head cocked and she asked, "Oh?"

"He disapproves heartily."

Violet's mouth twisted and she said, "Thank you for letting me know."

Lady Eleanor sipped her tea and then set it on the table next to her bed before she asked,

"So you'll be ending things, I assume."

Violet played with the ring on her finger. "Well, no. I like him very much. We are in the early days, and he may well lose interest when Victor and I leave for Bruges with Isolde, but I suspect that should he call again, I would be very amiably inclined to join him for dancing, indeed."

"Your father will hear of this," Lady Eleanor threatened.

"We have already spoken of it," Violet said simply and left so she didn't have to be there when her stepmother realized she'd been caught in a lie. Violet had never seen the way she used Father as a stick to prod the children along where she wanted them to go, but she suspected that she'd been the victim a time or two.

She made her way down the stairs and to the hall by the front door and found Victor with a bandaged hand and a scowl on his face.

"Were you magnificent?"

"Of course," he said. "Stings like the dickens."

Violet laughed. "It is a good thing we brought Giles to see us safely home. Injured as you were in the pursuit of truth. And what was the verdict?"

Victor scowled at Violet before he admitted, "Keeled over like a felled tree. Just as Father said."

"Let's go, shall we? I feel the need for fresh air."

Violet told him of her conversation with Lady Eleanor while they drove back to London. It was a long ride, and Violet had brought her journal with her. She sketched out her thoughts while Victor slept. Her original list of suspects had read:

Helen Mathers
Harry Mathers
Markus Kennington
Norman Kennington
Mr. Gulliver
Mr. Higgins
Hugo Danvers
Henry Carlyle

Violet ran over each of them in her mind. Helen Mathers, like Violet and Isolde, was too weak to have committed the crime. Given the way she'd tried to kill herself after his death, she must have had the final hope for a future fade with his death.

Harry Mathers was supposedly a good churchman who took careful care of his daughters beyond trusting his long-time partner too much with his child. If he did not realize the state of his daughter, why would he have killed Danvers? Unlike the rest of the people involved in the investment scheme, Mathers had a good likelihood of knowing that the scheme was a sham.

Violet had written a letter to Harry Mathers. She'd mentioned in that letter her concerns about his relationship with Danvers, but if she had been successful, Mathers had *brought* his daughter to the house where he would have murdered his partner.

Violet didn't see that as happening. Had he intended to challenge Danvers on the reality? Mathers had time enough to do that before the wedding day. If he had shown up intending to kill Danvers, he would have left his daughter home.

Violet very much wanted to talk to Helen. So many people knew of her existence as Danvers' lady friend. What had Helen known? She wasn't blind and dumb as people so often assumed of young girls like Helen. Violet made a wager with herself that she'd be able to get details from Helen that Mr. Barnes or Jack wouldn't be capable of getting Helen to reveal.

Markus Kennington was next on Violet's list. He hadn't been happy with Vi and Victor's questions, but Father's point about Markus's fortune weighed heavily on Vi's mind. The truth of the matter was that a man who had to button-up might give someone a good beating, but he wouldn't necessarily murder that person. That would ruin far more than economizing. His children were young. They weren't in a position of needing a start or even requiring very expensive schooling.

Violet played with her ring as she watched London take form. It was dank and grey that day, and she wanted to be at the sea. She sighed and glanced back down at her list. She felt certain that Victor's experiment vindicated Norman Kennington, especially since he hadn't lost everything. Like Markus, Norman might take a financial blow, but in the end, he'd be all right.

Mr. Gulliver. That one paused Violet. Mr. Fredericks had said that both Mr. Higgins and Mr. Gulliver were positioned to lose everything, and Violet had seen Mr. Gulliver physically pursuing Danvers. She couldn't remove him from her list.

She'd love to know what Jack had discovered about both Higgins and Gulliver, seeing as how she couldn't just show up at their house as she had done at the Matherses' house. Violet sighed. She was no more able to cross them off of her list than she was able to expand upon them.

But what about Hugo? Violet's first instinct was to circle his name and underline it. She knew, however, that was because she didn't like him. If she paused and considered his behavior, how much of his father's income had he been counting on inheriting? Did Hugo know it was all stolen? If the scheme failed, would Hugo be able to slide away with the stolen funds and leave everyone else with an empty bag?

The last name was her father, but Violet was certain that her father had not killed Danvers. He'd simply have ruined Danvers's good name and, in so doing, his business.

CHAPTER SEVENTEEN

Violet was dressing for an evening out when Isolde entered her bedroom. "I suppose it would be very improper of me to go dancing with you."

Violet grinned at her sister. "Well darling, it would be. You must pretend to mourn for at least two weeks. Surely by then, they'll have a good idea of who killed that blighter you escaped, and we'll be able to go on our trip. Did you start reading the book about Belgium?"

Isolde nodded and sat on the writing table where Violet's typewriter was covered and her journal was tucked into the drawer with her favorite pen. She looked rather glum as she watched Vi put on her finery.

"Dancing isn't a pastime that is going away, love. We'll go with you so often you'll be begging to remain abed with a treatise on manners and housekeeping."

Isolde's snort of laughter was just what Violet was looking for. She turned on the stool in front of her vanity and said, "Darling one, don't be sad."

"Oh, I suppose I'm not so sad. It's likely enough that I'd

get to the club and wish to go home and whimper into my pillow."

Violet laughed merrily and put on her makeup. She was wearing her kimono and Isolde exclaimed over it when Violet rose to examine her dresses. Violet pulled out a black dress with shimmering gold detailing. It had straps at the shoulders, a low waist, with a hem that was higher in the front than the back. It would show off her pretty diamond-buckled shoes.

The second option had lacy, sleeveless straps, jagged uneven hems that reached her midcalf only at the longest points, and it was entirely gold.

Vi loved them both but let Isolde choose, and she chose the gold dress, a braided gold headpiece with a peacock feather to one side, and gold and pearl ear bobs. Violet wrapped her favorite long strand of pearls around her neck a few times and added a diamond choker from Aunt Agatha's collection. With several diamond bracelets, Violet shimmered with each breath. "You look like Aphrodite or some other goddess," Isolde said with wide eyes.

Violet laughed and kissed each of her sister's cheeks before she put on red lipstick and placed a black and gold wrap around her shoulders.

"Thank you, darling," Vi said happily.

"Where will you go?"

"Oh, I don't know. Victor and Denny seem to have a mission to sleuth out the best places for jazz, drinks, and dancing. They do all right at it too."

Vi joined her brother in the foyer and he said, "The others will meet us there, luv. And don't you look like a golden drop of sunshine."

Vi grinned and replied, "You look rather smashing your-self. I am utterly thrilled to be escaping the gloom of this case. For the first time since we've been back to England, I feel as though we've come home."

Victor laughed.

They drove across London to a club where he'd reserved a table for them. They entered to a cloud of smoke and dim lights. Violet left her bag and shawl with the girl at the desk and then let her brother lead her through the crowd. It was noisy and smoke-filled but buzzed with an energy that had Violet bouncing on her toes as they were seated by a slender, black man with a magnificent set of eyebrows. She grinned at him, and he winked before leaving them at the table.

It took Violet a moment to realize that the form she'd thought at first was Denny was, in fact, Jack.

"Jack! You look dashing! I wasn't expecting you."

He'd already ordered drinks and handed her a gin and tonic with another for Victor. "I hope the surprise is acceptable?"

She laughed and nodded as the girl on the stage started a song that captured Violet's attention for a moment before she said, "Oh, isn't her voice lovely."

"I went ahead and ordered nibbles as well," Jack told Victor.

Her brother nodded but added to the order. "I might look slender, but I could always eat."

The first number ended and Jack pulled Vi onto the floor. She shivered in delight. They danced until she wasn't quite sure how much time had passed, but when he suggested stopping for a breather and a drink, she was famished for food and desperately thirsty.

When they returned to the table, it was empty, but she could see Victor dancing with a gorgeous blonde and Denny and Lila moving through the number with the grace of a couple who'd danced so often together, they could anticipate each other's every move.

Jack ordered drinks, and they decided to try something new. This time it was early spring berries muddled into a mint julep. The waiter said he'd heard it was good, with a waggle of his eyebrows, and they took his suggestion.

"Victor said you made your way back to Kennington House?" Jack asked and Violet nodded.

"Did he tell you anything else?"

Jack shook his head, so she told him of what she'd learned from Markus and Norman

Kennington, confirming Frederick's guess about their finances.

She retold Victor's dramatic tale of having borrowed a pocket knife off a gardener, hunting up Norman in the gardens, cutting his 'mortal flesh' and then attacking Norman with his bloody hand.

"He keeled right over. Papa described it as a tree being felled and Vic said it was just so."

By the end of the story, Jack was laughing and Violet had been presented with a plate of chocolate-covered strawberries and more lobster canapés. They shared the small plates and their fingers had somehow become tangled together under the table when Denny and Lila collapsed into their seats.

"Hot, isn't it?" Lila asked, reaching over and snagging one of the strawberries.

Lila inquired after the case as they ate and heard the update about Helen. Her gaze narrowed as she heard of Helen's fate told mostly in whispers while Jack and Denny discussed yachting.

"I'd buy a yacht," Denny said, loudly enough to catch Lila's attention. "But my wife won't let me."

Lila shot Denny a barely concealed irritation. "While we were gone, Denny spent too much time with Tomas St. Marks, who went from Paris to a ship-builder in Scotland and then sailed home on some sleek beauty."

"I thought you spent all your time eating your feelings, my friend?"

Denny snorted. "Well, I did that too. Look at this?" He stood and pointed out the bulging buttons on his vest. "Lila is going to have to dance with me for nights on end until I can wear this suit and breathe easily."

Violet rolled her eyes at him. "Tell Jack who you think killed Danvers."

"If it wasn't me? I was there you know, and the more I know of him, the more I hate him." Denny gestured to the waiter and ordered another round of drinks. He added to the order a series of finger foods before Victor returned to the table. He'd brought his dance partner back to her friends and settled in with his sister and their friends.

"What are we talking about?" he asked.

"Murders," Denny said. "So we've got more booze on the way. The jazz makes it seem less...real."

"According to Vi, it was about as real as it gets, my friend. You can tell when Vi thinks about it because she changes colors."

Denny and Victor turned to Jack, who was the only other one who'd actually seen the body. He sighed. "The killer seemed angry."

Violet shuddered. "Can we not talk about that part of it?"

"Seconded," Lila said.

"Where's Gwennie?"

"Dinner with the aunt," Denny said. "Who do you think did the deed, Victor?"

"My money is on Gulliver. He's gonna lose everything, he was getting a bit physical with Danvers before the chappie died, and I didn't like his expression when he was trying to trick Vi into throwing her fortune down the crapper after his."

They all looked to Jack, who scowled at each of them in turn.

"Well?" Lila's expression was an out and out dare.

Jack sighed. "I haven't decided. I lean towards Gulliver myself. Barnes tracked down Mathers today, but he went straight home after, so I haven't heard the details there. Higgins has an alibi. Norman Kennington will be more affected by the losses than Markus, but given his reaction to the blood today, it seems unlikely that he'd have been able to murder Danvers in the way he was killed."

"What about Hugo?" Vi asked as she sipped her drink. Denny had ordered this round, and they'd all gotten flutes of champagne.

"You just hate him," Victor told Vi.

She considered and then nodded. "All the same...he's got my vote for the killer."

They all glanced back to Jack.

"The motive for him is tenuous," Jack told them. "Why would he kill his father? Why at that time? With so many people around?"

"Perhaps for just that reason," Violet said. "If he killed his father at home, it narrows the pool considerably, doesn't it?"

Jack grinned at Violet. "I need fresh air."

"Shall we go back to the house? We can make 2:00 a.m. sandwiches. Ham, cheese, watercress."

"Please, feed me," Denny pled. "Lila has taken away all the good things." He popped the last of the canapés in his mouth. "I need something more than mouthfuls."

"It would cheer Isolde if we went back there for drinks. Assuming she isn't already asleep. I had Giles get her some sleeping pills, so she's starting to look a little better." "And yet she's so pale and wan." Victor sighed. "I wonder if Bruges will be enough."

"She's young," Jack said. "She'll recover. It's been but days, my friends. She is lucky. She has you and your sister. And your oldest brother and your father are both more concerned for her than anything else. I've worked enough of these cases to know how lucky your sister is."

Violet rode back to her house with Jack.

"I didn't realize Victor hadn't told you I was invited," he confessed.

Violet laughed. "Victor approves of you. His machinations are his way of showing it."

"I don't want to suffocate you. If you'd like, we can adjust our plans for the Criterion and the play."

Vi grinned at him. "You *did,* however, already buy play tickets?"

"Barnes would be happy enough to go in our place, if..."

"Jack, I am going to be very straightforward with you for a moment and set aside the games we ladies like to play with you gents."

He glanced at her, his lips twitching. "I think I'm ready for this great revelation."

"If I didn't want to join you for dinner, I would tell you so. If I hadn't wanted to ride with you in this car and to spend more time with you, I'd have gone with Victor."

"Let me see if I can translate the female speak you just gave me."

"Ah!" Violet said, "You fiend! Translate then—"

"You are, in fact, willing to go to dinner with me tomorrow and to the play?"

Violet nodded. "Did you wish to escape me? Perhaps you're just trying to put the blame of canceling on me?"

"Indeed not," Jack replied and somehow their fingers tangled together again.

When they reached Victor's house, Vi found Isolde wearing her kimono and learning from Victor how to make drinks.

"Scandalous minx!" Vi scolded playfully. "I'd tell you to

throw a dress on, but I suppose you are showing less skin than I."

"I should have asked. I just wanted to see what it felt like."

"Think nothing of it," Violet told Isolde. "You look splendid in gold and black!"

CHAPTER EIGHTEEN

Violet had a determined lie-in the next morning, but she wasn't able to sleep as she'd planned. Instead, she found herself flipping through her journal. First, she wrote about Jack, and she had to admit she was looking forward to donning that black and gold evening gown and sitting in the theater with him. The sheer idea that he wanted to spend his time with her left her quite distracted.

Violet flipped from the history of her and Jack. Their interactions were so few that she had to remind herself that she didn't have enough experience with him to be anything other than infatuated.

When she avoided the sections about Jack, the rest was about Isolde, both before and after the murder, and what Violet had found out about Danvers. She wanted, no needed, to hear a perspective of a woman who wanted to be around him. She could imagine how Isolde had tried to be blind to much of what occurred around Danvers, but would it be the same with Helen?

Margate wasn't so far from London. If they took an early

train, she and Victor could go down, see Helen and Mr. Mathers, and return in time for the late dinner and play.

Vi rang the bell for Beatrice.

"My lady?"

"Send Giles in to Victor. Tell Victor to wake and dress. Wear a casual suit. We're going to the sea."

Beatrice's brows rose and she asked, "Do you need me to pack you a trunk?"

"No, no, we'll be back by the evening train. Hurry now."

Violet washed quickly, dressed, and harassed the still-shaving Victor through finishing dressing. They ate a quick breakfast and had Giles drive them to the train station, just barely making the late morning train. The journey was quiet as Violet considered her notes again and again.

Mr. Gulliver, Mr. Mathers, and Hugo Danvers.

What was Jack doing to pursue Mr. Gulliver? Did he have anything that would provide the man an alibi or a reason to have killed? What about Hugo? People were there to celebrate his own father's wedding. Surely someone had seen him during the window when the murder occurred?

Violet found herself distracted from her thoughts about the murder to consider the role of a female in all this. Vi pictured Helen, Isolde, and herself and the different lives they'd had already. Then Vi added in Gwennie and Lila. Each of the women lived in a time when women had more freedom than ever before. They were, however, facing the same issues that women had faced for generations.

Helen had been lied to and manipulated by a man who had claimed to love her. Lila had married her long-time love and found herself happiness that was fraught with frustration only because she and Denny insisted on going their own path while everyone around them was waiting to hear an announcement that included little bundles of joy and less jazz.

Gwennie was reliant on the generosity of her family but

also controlled by their expectations. If Gwennie could have worked without causing a huge ruckus in her family, she would have. They wanted her, however, beholden to them and behaving as they chose.

Then there was Isolde, the long-time spoiled daughter of an earl who was manipulated and pushed into an engagement that was the antithesis of everything she'd ever wanted for herself. Pursuing an education wasn't necessary, nothing was but attaching herself to a rich man and letting him see to her needs.

And then there was Vi. She'd been able to have much more freedom than the rest, but mostly because her eccentricities always included Victor. Vi had the protection of a man with the assumption of others that he controlled her. If she hadn't had Victor, would Violet have been treated as another carefree chit who'd thrown away the wisdom of the ages?

Yet here she was—with all this freedom—and still finding herself dreaming of love, a home, and marriage. Was it the feminine in her? Perhaps women were born desiring these things? Or perhaps it was simply the effect of Jack on her?

Vi laid her head on her brother's shoulder and watched the country pass by, wondering about all of the women who were on the other side of the glass going about their lives. Just because the right to vote had been extended to women—and not even Violet yet—it didn't mean that they'd truly found equality.

"You seem very serious," Victor said.

"I..."

Victor waited, lips twitching, and she knew he was using her favorite interrogation technique on her. She scowled at him, and he grinned back.

"I find myself confused by my reaction to Jack."

"Why?"

The best thing about having a twin brother who had always seen her as the better piece of himself was that she knew he'd understand.

"I feel like it's going too fast between us."

"Darling Vi," Victor said, "realizing you enjoy Jack's company and that you're attracted to him does not mean that you have committed your days to him."

"It's going too fast inside my head," she admitted. "It's just that I find my mind wondering what that would be like. I go there again and again in my mind, and it's driving me mad."

Victor laughed. "You always were a planner. You think and examine and try things out with your imagination. What's terrifying is not trying Jack out in your mind, silly girl. What's terrifying you is that for the first time—when you imagine a future with someone else—you are *not* tempted to run away."

Violet licked her lips. Was Victor right? He usually was when it came to understanding her. Perhaps the problem was that she was prepared to imagine a future with a man and feel that she could never abide it. She knew what to do with those feelings and how to handle that reaction. What did you do with something different? She hadn't been prepared for that at all.

A 'no' was perhaps, far, far easier than a 'yes.' Yeses were less safe. They required more work. More trust in yourself. Actually trusting, truly and completely, and that person being anyone other than Victor. Vi wasn't all that sure she had that much capacity for faith in someone else.

"Vi," Victor said gently. "Do you know why Denny and Lila work so perfectly?"

She shook her head.

"Because they got to the point where the image of a future without each other was untenable. They'd rather struggle together than apart. You'll know when a future with Jack is the right thing when you want it more than you want your safety net. Until then? Have fun. You haven't yet made promises nor are you being asked to do so."

Violet nodded and then pulled her journal back out, writing out her thoughts about what Victor had suggested. That, she thought, she could do. She could wait until when she imagined a future without Jack in it—and it wasn't one she could abide.

She didn't have to decide if she was in love at that moment. Not this moment, this day or even this year. She didn't have to decide if she was falling in love. She could, instead, try to figure out how she would know. It was enough to say she enjoyed his company. Vi liked how Jack made her feel, and she was happy to keep on considering him.

———

"There is something about the sea that makes the day seem brighter," Violet told Victor as he put up the umbrella they'd purchased and placed it over the both of them.

He laughed at her but didn't discount her theory. It was the same for him. It always had been. The sound of the sea, the call of the gulls, the scent of salt and wet in the air—they always made things better for the twins.

They had the name of the place where Mr. Mathers and Helen were staying, but as they walked through the town, Violet nudged Victor. "There's Helen."

Helen had gone from pale and upset to death walking. The circles under her eyes were huge, and she sat in a tearoom with a pot of tea and a plate of biscuits in front of her, but they were untouched. She sat alone, and she was staring out the window of the tearoom but didn't seem to be seeing the scene in front of her.

Violet knew without speaking to Helen that she'd never reveal a thing of the womanly nature with Victor present.

"Track down Mr. Mathers?" Vi suggested. "He'll talk to you more frankly without me there, and I believe it'll be the same with Helen."

Victor nodded. "I'll come find you here. Don't go off without me."

She agreed, and he left her while she went into the tearoom and seated herself with Helen.

It took Helen a few moments to realize that she'd been invaded, and when she did, she squeaked.

"I'm sorry," Vi told her. "I didn't mean to scare you. I just saw you sitting here..."

"Please don't," Helen said, holding up a hand. "I know you tracked me down. I got a letter from Anna. I know that you found out all my secrets."

It hadn't been well done of Vi to manipulate Anna as she had, but there was a murderer afoot and two of the main suspects had disappeared. There had to be a point where that was more important than what Helen preferred.

Violet crossed her fingers together in her lap. "The puzzle of who killed Danvers is occupying my thoughts and preventing my sister from moving on. It's not only you who needs closure. We all do."

Helen's expression said she wasn't all that invested in what burden Isolde might be carrying or the turn of Violet's thoughts.

"It's not her fault, you know," Violet tried. Maybe if she made Isolde human to Helen, the girl would realize that they were both victims.

"That she stole Carlton from me?"

"That Carlton and my stepmother determined the match and manipulated her into it."

Helen scoffed and played with her teacup. "She knew of me," Helen told Violet without an ounce of sympathy for Isolde. "I found your sister myself, told her that Carlton had promised to marry me, told her he convinced me to bed him based off of that promise."

Violet played with her ring, wincing for both Helen and Isolde.

Helen sniffed, placing a hand over her stomach as she said, "If you are expecting me to set aside my own concerns to worry over your sister, I'm afraid I don't have it in me."

Violet realized that for Helen, Isolde would always be part of the reason of why Helen's fate shifted. There wasn't going to be some quick-witted comment or series of leading questions that made Helen change her mind. So how to get her help? What did she need?

The answer came so suddenly to Vi that she was speaking before she thought it through.

"What if I were to offer you a quiet villa by the sea on the Amalfi coast? It is private, far from here, has a wonderful view. It's very sunny in Italy. It would be easy enough to bring a midwife masquerading as a maid and hide yourself away until a certain day arrives."

Helen's mouth twisted. "My secrets for a refuge?"

"The full use of the villa for a year in exchange for whatever you know about Danvers.

You could bring your sister."

"What do I do with the"—Helen struggled for a moment —"bundle?"

That Violet wasn't so sure of. Did Helen search for a good home? Did she try to find some childless couple that would take the babe in? Did she persuade her father to take on the child? Did she keep it herself and face being ostracized?

"What do you want to do?"

Helen's laugh was humorless. "Go back in time and never go out of the house with Carlton Danvers. Scream and throw a fit when my father suggested it. I grabbed at the opportunity like a drowning person a life preserver."

Violet winced. Not for what had happened so much as for the self-loathing in Helen's voice. "I wish I could make that possible for you."

Helen snorted in reply.

Violet considered. The question of the child's fate was one that she didn't feel qualified to comment on. But it wasn't going to go away. "Do you feel love for the baby?"

Helen took in a slow breath. "Yes and no. I see her in my mind. This little person. When I imagine her, she's always a girl. My goodness, Violet, I hate her father. Despise him so much I wish I was the one who struck the killing blow. I hate that she exists. I hate myself for letting it come to this."

"So you don't want her?" Violet nudged Helen as the waitress approached and the conversation halted while Violet ordered tea and scones.

"Oh, I want her." Helen teared up. "But she deserves better than me. Yet I also don't want her because of all she represents."

"You could love her. You could raise her. You could take care of her. Find a little village. Be a widow."

Helen nodded. "I won't risk my hatred for her father ruining her life. What if, when she arrives, I can't move past it? What if I can't love her as she deserves? She's the biggest victim here. Unwanted from the moment of her conception. I love her enough to have her. I want what is best for her, and it's not me. Yet, how do I entrust her to someone else?"

It was a question that Violet didn't have the experience to answer.

"Would you accept the villa and allow me to have someone look into it? See if I can find some family that will look past her origins and love her as she deserves to be loved?"

Helen couldn't hold back a tear as she asked, "Do you

think it's possible to love a child that isn't your own? As though they were?"

Violet honored the mother inside of Helen and then answered her honestly. "After my mother died, Victor and I were raised mostly by my mother's aunt. There was never a day when we felt unloved by her or loved less than other children."

"But you were her kin."

"I suppose that's true enough. But I don't believe that was why she loved us. She loved us because she..." Violet paused before continuing. "I think it is human nature to love and be loved. She loved us because we were hers to care for and love. She loved us because we needed her to. She loved us because people who are good love those they care for and protect."

"Will you find someone and make sure that they love her?"

Violet nodded.

"Why am I trusting you with this?" Helen demanded, and then she answered her own question. "Because who else will help me?"

A moment later after they'd both topped off their tea and crumbled a scone without eating a bite, Helen said, "What do you need to know?"

CHAPTER NINETEEN

"Did you know that Danvers was stealing money from those who invested with him?"

Helen's jaw dropped and she shook her head. "Do you think my father was stealing as well?"

Violet nodded and Helen's mouth trembled as she stared without comprehension at Violet.

Finally, Helen said, "Father used to tell me, when I asked for something frivolous, that I didn't understand how hard he worked to provide. What he sacrificed to make sure I was secure. I...my goodness Violet, why would he have said that if he wasn't stealing. I also thought it was odd. What the devil? Are all men untrustworthy?"

Violet didn't answer. It wasn't as though Helen would accept Violet's opinion on the matter.

"What do you know of Mr. Gulliver?"

Helen stared at her teacup. "He was always rude to me. Treated me like a two-bit whore." Her hands trembled as she brought her teacup to her mouth. "I should have known how

Carlton was talking about me if his friends treated me that way."

"You should have," Violet told her. "It's good that you're young and beautiful. You'll have a chance to judge better next time."

Helen laughed despite herself. "You're not kind at all, are you? That was utterly without sympathy."

Vi's brows rose. "I might feel far more sorry for you if you were homely or truly loved Carlton. But you didn't."

"I didn't."

"Then I won't lie to you to make you feel better. That's how women like us get into these messes. Our friends are so worried about our feelings in the moment, they don't stop to think that the truth is far kinder than a well-meant lie. We're not, after all, talking about fringe or no fringe or the way a dress you love wears. We're talking about things that lead you to where you are today."

Helen sighed and then looked at Violet almost wonderingly. "I wish you'd been there to knock some sense into me."

Vi twisted her ring around her finger then rearranged the items on their table as she thought about what else she needed to know.

"Mr. Gulliver invested, so Mr. Danvers couldn't have been all that big of a friend of his."

Helen thought back. "Well. Yes. That is true. Carlton used to make little asides about him.

They were always quite mean."

Violet played with her ring some more and then asked, "Were you with your father for the whole of the wedding?"

Helen's head cocked. "You think Papa might have killed Carlton?"

"How would your father feel if he found out that his long-time business partner, entrusted to take his beloved daughter about town, had used that opportunity to romance, manipulate, and impregnate her before throwing her over for a better-connected quarry?" "I don't have to wonder that," Helen said. "He'll rage. Then stare out the window without hearing your comments. You'll hear him crying at night, and you'll know that your actions— stupid as they were—devastated your father. Maybe ruined him."

Violet reached out then; she couldn't stop herself. She took Helen's hand, hoping she wasn't pushing too far. "I'm sure he blames himself as well."

"He does! Yet another thing to hate myself for." Helen searched Vi's face. "My father didn't kill Carlton. If he'd known my situation, these last days wouldn't have been like they are. I have no doubt of it. Papa didn't know. If he didn't know about me and he was helping *with the stealing* for years, why would he murder his partner?"

Violet picked up her teacup and took a long drink. Helen wasn't going to adjust that story. Vi wasn't sure she could believe it. It was clear that Helen loved her father and felt guilty. If lying to protect him would do so, Helen would swear the moon was made of cheese and we all lived on the back of a giant turtle—whatever was necessary.

Helen could guess the direction of Violet's thoughts. "Father never left me the whole time we were at the wedding."

Such an easy lie.

"Just after we ran into you," Helen continued, "Father met an old business friend. Oliver Jones. He works for the Bank of England, and we didn't leave him either. We were seated together, and Father and Mr. Jones discussed business while I tried to stifle my tears about what to do. Mr. Jones noticed I wasn't well and asked after me. He was quite concerned, I think, that I was ill and catching. He'll tell you. He and Father knew each other from school, not recently.

They aren't so close that they'd lie for each other now."

That changed everything, didn't it? Mr. Mathers had been Violet's primary suspect. The list of suspects narrowed in Violet's mind. The details of Helen's father's distraction were verifiable with servants. The friend could provide an alibi. If Mr. Mathers was removed as the suspect, that left only Mr. Gulliver and Hugo Danvers.

"Tell me about Hugo," Violet said, leaving the question open so that her prejudices didn't affect the manner in which Helen spoke of him.

"Oh." Helen shuddered. "He's not right."

"What do you mean?"

"He...it seems as though he felt he was competing with Carlton. Not that they were father and son, but that they were rivals. They hated each other. Carlton hated Hugo, and the reverse was as true."

"With you too? Did Hugo attempt to..." Vi didn't bother providing details. There was no question what Vi meant.

Helen shuddered again and nodded. Vi didn't press her further. But Helen asked, "Was it the same with Isolde?"

Violet was the one who shuddered and nodded that time, and the two of them stared at each other.

There were a few things that Victor would never understand about Vi simply because she was a woman and he a man, but this was something that every woman could understand on the behalf of the other.

"What does he do for a living? Did Carlton support him?"

Helen's laugh was mean as she shook her head. "I believe he gambled."

"To live?"

"He went to special places for gamblers. Carlton talked about them. Hugo used to make these comments to Carlton about how bad he was at gambling and then Carlton would get angry.

He was always meaner after that. It felt like there was more to know than he'd talk about."

Violet ordered another pot of tea and plate of sandwiches for them, and this time they'd both found their appetites. Helen had taken only a few bites of her smoked salmon sandwich when something else occurred to her.

"Hugo was angry with his father about Isolde. For a while, I wanted to believe it was because of me. But I think…"

Helen hesitated and Violet leaned forward. "*All* of your secrets about this. A villa for a year isn't something you'll get from anyone else. Your father just might send you to a home for unwed mothers."

Helen shuddered and cleared her throat. "I'm not trying to protect myself. I'm just not sure *why* it happened the way it did."

"Tell me," Violet insisted and Helen shrugged.

"Hugo was upset about Carlton's engagement to Isolde. Furious even. The fight between them wasn't even close to normal. The one time they discussed it, it had been when Carlton took me to a play. They were yelling at each other in the hallway and we were all asked to leave. It was embarrassing. Even worse, Hugo was so angry it was alarming. I was worried that he'd actually attack his father."

"What the devil?" Vi breathed and Helen nodded.

"I was still hoping that Carlton wasn't serious about Isolde, so I suggested that he consider whether he really wanted to destroy what remained of his relationship with his son, but Carlton laughed. Said he was pursuing Isolde for the business connections, but Hugo's reaction made it all the sweeter." Helen laughed an angry little sound. "That was when I still allowed myself to believe that it was all lies, and he'd get the business connections and investments and leave her for me."

"Hugo seems to be preoccupied with my sister," Vi told

Helen, who couldn't help but shiver in sympathy. Isolde might have 'stolen' Carlton from Helen, but still, the girl found sympathy when it came to Hugo.

They finished their tea and Violet spoke again. "I don't know what will happen to your father in the coming months as the financial crimes that Carlton was a part of come to light. If you need help in getting a new start after your trip to the Amalfi Coast, you are not alone."

Helen nodded, seeming emotional for a moment, and then she left Violet. Vi lingered over another pot of tea, sipping slowly. When Victor appeared an hour later, he ordered a bundle of sandwiches to go and they hurried to catch the next train out of Margate.

"Mathers has an alibi," Victor told Vi, who nodded.

"So I understand," Vi answered.

Vi told Victor what she'd learned and his brows rose as he heard Vi's offer to use the villa while Helen had her lying-in.

Victor also learned that Hugo was a bounder. But he further learned that when Mr.

Mathers had started to work with Danvers, things had been on the up and up. It was only after Danvers lost everything in a series of gambling failures that he'd started these investment schemes.

Mr. Mathers insisted that he'd only helped with the legitimate side of the business, but Victor seemed to disbelieve the man. Violet wasn't sure what she believed, but if Helen was being honest, Vi was pretty sure Helen—like Victor—believed that Mr. Mathers was in deep.

"The poor blighter," Vic said. "He seemed a little baffled by his life even as he was lying to me about what he knew."

Victor and Violet eventually fell into silence. Violet pulled out her journal once again. She wrote for a while before she said, "I wish we could get what Jack knows about Gulliver. I feel certain we'd know who killed Mr. Danvers if we had details about that man."

"Let's invite him to our place for pre-dinner drinks, love. I'll grill him and you sit and look pretty and admiring. He won't be able to help himself to reveal all he knows in the face of our joint efforts."

"I know we don't know all that much about Mr. Gulliver, but Victor...I don't like Hugo. Killer or not, he needs to stay away from Isolde."

CHAPTER TWENTY

The door was open to their house when they arrived and the twins glanced at each other before hurrying up the front walk. Whatever was happening?

The front hall held Hargreaves, their brother Gerald, Isolde, Beatrice, Giles, and the local bobby.

"What's all this?" Victor asked as he set down his hat, gaze fixed on the policeman.

Violet slipped off her coat and her cloche and noticed that Isolde was a little pale, but she didn't seem overly upset.

"Someone tried to force entry into your house, old man," Gerald said. "The servants were all out and I had taken Isolde to lunch and a little outing. When we got back the bobbies were here and all was in a tizzy."

Victor's brows rose and he asked Hargreaves, "Did they get in?"

"No, sir," Hargreaves said as he closed the front door. "The footman from next door noticed something was amiss and chased the blighter off."

Victor frowned and turned to the policeman while Vi said,

"If we've avoided disaster, I'll just run upstairs and get dressed."

Isolde shook her head and handed Violet a note with her name on it. She'd seen glimpses of Jack's notebook enough to recognize his handwriting. It was with a frown that she took the note.

It was, she knew, an ominous sign. Vi tossed the group a grin and a wink to cover her concern. "I'll leave you to it."

She skipped up to her room and opened the door. She glanced into her jewelry box. Nothing was amiss. Any concern that they'd actually been burgled faded. She'd left rather a lot of expensive jewelry outside of the safe. A laziness she'd need to correct.

Violet needed to read the note, but she felt the ominous brush of wondering. Had Jack intended to cancel the date yesterday by giving her an escape from the dinner and play? If he had, how foolish she'd looked when she'd told him that she wouldn't play the games women played.

Violet slowly opened the note and read:

Violet—
    I am unable to attend the dinner and play this evening.
    Jack

What was she supposed to do with a note like this? Violet threw it to the side. A part of her wanted to pull out her journal and scribble all her feelings down, but they were too rambunctious even for that. Rather than get dressed, Violet threw her things to the side, stared at the mess for a moment and then hung up her clothes. The sight of them strewn about was making her fingers itchy.

She started a bath, playing with a combination of salts and bath oils, so her very skin would smell like a garden. She slid into the water, and when her mind wouldn't stop racing, she slid under the water, holding her breath tightly. The pressure on her lungs drew attention from her doubts until she finally pushed from the water to tell herself, "You're being ridiculous."

Violet worked soap into her hair and then the sponge to run it over her limbs. "So, your date got canceled. That's hardly something to have a fizz up about."

Violet finished her bath, wrapped herself up in a nightgown and a kimono and made her way down to the dining room. Cook hadn't been expecting them to stay in. Would they even have dinner?

"What's all this?" Victor asked. "Don't you have dinner plans? I tried to get Jack to come hear what we've learned, but he can't be located."

She smiled brightly, making herself a drink, as Victor followed her through the house.

"He canceled. I thought I'd work on our story and..."

Victor laughed. "So you thought you'd put on a bright face and I wouldn't notice that you'd suddenly decided that your kimono was outerwear and that you wanted a...is that a bee's knees?"

Violet turned and raised a brow, holding up the bottle of gin. "Did you want one?"

"Yes, darling, I want one. As does Isolde. But you, old thing, don't get to bounce around here pretending you aren't in a fizz."

Violet put less gin in his bee's knees after that. He noticed, taking hers instead.

"You're a devil."

"You don't have your best actress foot forward, love. Let's see it now. I would say I feel terribly bad about leaving you behind, but I'm off to meet up with Tomas."

Violet shot Victor a narrowed gaze.

"I know already that you'd like to avoid his company since

he has yet to propose to you again this year."

She cocked her head and sipped deeply from her bee's knees. "Oh, that's sweet."

"Just the thing you need right now. To help balance out the sour you're pretending not to have. That chocolate liqueur we bought in Paris arrived today while we were gone. Some of the other things we bought might..."

Violet turned to Victor. "I love you, brother. But, go away. You're trying to give me a list of things to distract me. Go and have a drink with Tomas, listen to some music, eat some food, indulge your senses. I can take care of myself."

Victor grinned at Violet. "Well now. You *are* in a fizz. I told you so."

"You, sir, will be in a fizz if you don't leave me be."

He escaped, but a few minutes later Isolde came in with a careful expression on her face.

"Oh, stop it." Violet pulled all the bottles of alcohol from their cart and was examining them. "I'm fine."

"Of course you are. Why wouldn't you be?" Isolde sounded a little like a parrot, speaking the one phrase it had been taught without any of the right tones.

Violet shot Isolde a mocking glance. "Ring for someone and turn on the wireless. We're going to be giddy."

Isolde watched as Violet started opening bottles and sniffing them, putting them in inexplicable arrangements.

"What are you doing?"

"Playing," Violet said and then when a song came on that she liked, Violet spun with the bottle in her hand.

"What is that you've got there?"

"Limoncello. Victor loves to buy alcohol. He buys it wherever we go. He'll probably buy cases of Belgium beer and genever while we're in Bruges. He'll send some home to Father, some to Gerald, and stock his own ridiculous collection. While we were gone, he bought chocolate liqueur in

France." Vi tapped the top of one fanciful bottle and winked at Isolde, who looked suddenly intrigued.

Violet poured a little of the limoncello into two glasses and added some of the chocolate liqueur to one and some ginger wine to another.

"Whatever are you doing?" Isolde asked, watching Violet take a sip of one of the glasses and make a face. Vi handed the glass to her sister and tried the next one.

"I've always loved ginger wine," Vi told Isolde, setting aside the two drinks she mixed, as well as her bee's knees, and took a fresh glass and poured herself the ginger wine.

"Do you?" Isolde kept the limoncello and chocolate cocktail and sipped it. "I always assumed you just liked cocktails."

Violet shrugged and admitted, "Oh I do. I like how creative they are. I learn how to make the ones I like. But sometimes, I just want a little glass of ginger wine, a good book, and maybe some chocolate."

"You," Isolde told her sister, "are blue and pretending not to be. Do you like Mr.
Wakefield that much?"

Violet nodded as Beatrice opened the door in response to the bell.

"Darling, I know Cook expected us to be out, but we'll be in. Will you bring us something to eat? Anything?"

"He cooked for Lady Isolde, m'lady. Did you want a tray?"

"Two trays. We're going to listen to the wireless and ignore that there is quite a lovely dining room in this house."

Violet changed the subject as soon as Beatrice left and once she was back with the food, Violet nibbled on it, sipped her single glass of ginger wine, and listened to the music with her feet up.

"I would like a kimono," Isolde said after a long while. She'd cleaned up the mess Violet had made with the bar, letting her sister snuggle into the comfortable chair. "Perhaps we might go shopping tomorrow?"

"Yes, I'll be done with my mope tomorrow and prepared to force clothes upon you. It won't be necessary for anyone to press clothes upon me as acquiring them is as natural as breathing."

Isolde laughed as Violet curled onto her side and fell asleep listening to the music. Isolde woke her not long after and got Vi up to her room where she slept the megrims away.

————

Victor woke Violet the next morning.

"I have the vaguest memory of having done something horrible."

Violet pushed up her eye mask and scowled at her brother. "I was going to have a lie-in."

"I dove right into my cups with Tomas. He was upset about you, I was upset about Jack leaving you with half a note, we indulged."

Vi's gaze narrowed on Victor's.

"Of course, I snuck in here and read it. Don't be slow, luv."

Violet pulled her eye mask the rest of the way off and pushed herself up. Her steely gaze was doing nothing to cow her brother.

"Tomas was glummer than you were, love. We got well and thoroughly toasted without nearly as many nibbles as you and I usually order. I recall finding out where Jack lived. And then...did I go there?"

Violet's mouth dropped open and she took her pillow to beat at her brother.

"I know, I know, but mercy. My head, Vi. My head!"

"Find him," she ordered. "Find Jack and make it better. Whatever you did, undo!"

"By Jove, I will. I swear I will. I'll find his place again. How did I find it drunk? I'll explain that Tomas alone is like drinking with a fish. You are required to dance with him, so he doesn't drown in gin."

"Jack!" Vi cut in.

"Somehow it'll make it all my fault. I was angry, you will have been all smiles."

"Not smiles!" Vi said. "A little disappointed, but not shaken. Still clever. I went out with the girls. I didn't miss a beat."

Victor laughed. "Of course, you did! Why would a bright young thing like yourself stay home, make a mess in the bar, mix random drinks, and then console herself with ginger wine, the drink you prefer when you're glum."

Violet hit Victor with the pillow again and said, "Isolde and I are on a mission to acquire her a kimono."

"That fiend!" Victor said and then held his head at the sound of his own voice.

"We'll buy whatever we might need for Belgium."

"So, nothing? Because certainly, your wardrobe is sufficient for the entirety of the globe."

Violet ignored that comment. "After which, Isolde and I will have luncheon together and return home to a contrite brother who has made things right and is repentant. Perhaps in the mood to buy us both dinner at the Savoy."

"I'll make a reservation before I go."

"See that you do," Violet told him and then curled onto her side. "Ring for Beatrice on your way out. I think Isolde may have had all the things I mixed. She'll need Giles's concoction, aspirin, and probably some toast to soak up whatever booze is left in her stomach."

"The poor bug," Victor said. "I'll be needing all those things myself to mend whatever I did."

CHAPTER TWENTY-ONE

Finding a kimono was easy given the infatuation that the British currently had with all things Asian.

Isolde moaned over two until Violet purchased them both with a second for herself. Vi selected a scarlet kimono with dragons embroidered on it. Her acquisitive soul demanded it the moment Vi set her eyes on it.

"Vi," Isolde breathed, "look at this dress."

Violet paused and walked towards it. From a distance, it was a simple nude beige dress. But as you approached the details appeared. Shimmering gold beading, lacy accents, fringe that lengthened the line of the body.

"Oh my," Violet said.

"There's a matching gold shimmer wrap," the salesgirl said. "A headpiece too, if you like those."

"You have to try it on," Isolde said.

"We can adjust it to you specifically," the girl said. "I agree. This color of nude would look amazing on your skin."

Violet wasn't difficult to persuade. She stepped out of the dressing room and turned in front of the paneled mirror, running her hands down her body. She didn't need Isolde to say Vi looked amazing. She knew she did.

"She'll take it," Isolde said for Violet. The salesgirl sent for the seamstress, a woman about Vi's age of Asian descent. Her dark brown eyes sparkled as she examined Vi in the mirror. "You look lovely. It'll take at least three days for the adjustments. When they're done, we'll have it delivered. If you'd like a second fitting instead, I can bring it, but you'll find it's perfect."

"I'm sure it will be. We've heard the most wonderful things about your establishment," Violet said. "I'll pay, Isolde, if you want to look in at the hat shop? You said your cloche got crushed."

Her sister nodded, looking excited for another hat while Violet spoke with the seamstress.

"The designer is working on a dress that is garnet. It would require much daring to wear.

I'll have her pin it for your measurements and bring it when I come. You'll want it," the girl said.

Vi grinned at the woman and asked, "What is your name?"

"Liu Rushi."

"I sense a partnership?"

"Indubitably," Rushi replied with a wink, and Violet requested their purchases to be delivered.

Violet meandered her way to the hat shop several doors down.

Had Victor been able to sort things out with Jack without making Vi seem like some sort of obsessive female who'd been destroyed by a simple missed date? If so, how had he done it?

The door over the shop jangled and Vi stepped in, glancing around.

"What can I help you with? Perhaps a new hat to match that lovely coat?"

"I..." Vi slowly turned. The hat shop wasn't large and Isolde should be there. "I was supposed to be meeting my sister in here, only..."

"No one has come in for the last half hour," the man said.

Violet frowned. "Excuse me."

She glanced down the street and saw other women shopping. There was a cab a few shops down. The sidewalks were mostly empty and Vi saw no sign of her sister. Slowly she moved to the next store to see if Isolde had been distracted into that shop, but her attention was caught by an alleyway between that shop and the hat shop.

Isolde had been carrying a leather handbag and two little urchins were digging through it. "Hello there," Violet said to them, eye on the bag.

The smaller one let go of the bag and darted away, but Violet was able to catch the arm of the one closer.

"Let me go!"

"Stop struggling. Keep the bag, I don't care. I'll give you more money if you stop."

Slowly the child stopped struggling and Violet said, "Now. If you will swear to me that you won't run, I'll let go of you and pull out the money in my bag."

"You'll call the police."

"I won't," Vi swore. "I'll pinky swear."

The kid searched Vi's face and then slowly nodded and Violet let go of the child. She hesitated to step back until she saw the kid wasn't moving. It took a moment for Vi to realize, but the child was a girl! Vi held out her pinky and the girl curled a dirty digit around Vi's.

"Did you see what happened to the woman who was carrying this bag?"

The child nodded and Vi pulled out her pocketbook and grabbed blindly at the cash.

"Tell me," Vi ordered.

The child hesitated and Vi said, "Look at all this ready money." Violet rubbed it between her fingers so the stack of it could be seen.

"A man grabbed 'er."

"What did he look like?"

"Fancy bloke like you. Brown suit."

Violet thought back to who might have taken her and the only possibility was Hugo Danvers. "Did he have anything unusual about his face?"

The girl tapped the spot on her cheek where Hugo's large mole resided.

Violet moaned a little. "It's all right," she told herself.

"She didn't want to go," the girl told Vi, searching Violet's face.

"It's all right," Vi corrected, "because knowing who has my sister makes it easier to find her."

Vi gave the girl a card for her house and the money. "We're bound now, you and I," Vi said. "You've done me a good turn. One I can never repay. If you need help, that's where you'll find me. Tell Hargreaves I sent you, show him the card, and even if I'm not there, you'll be safe."

The girl nodded. She offered Vi Isolde's purse. Vi opened it, took out Isolde's money and gave it to the girl as well.

"I'm Violet," she said.

"Ginny."

"We're friends now," Violet told her. "Where can I find the local bobby?"

It was evident that the girl didn't want to say, but she led Vi through the streets of London using paths no one but a local would know. They poured out in a park where the bobby was walking and swinging his billy club.

"There he is," the girl said, stepping back.

Vi squeezed her shoulder, not letting go and called, "Help! Help, police!"

The girl squirmed but didn't try to run and the man came running.

"This girl steal from you?" he asked, his gaze narrowed.

"My sister was taken off the street. Ginny saw everything. We need help. We need...we need Mr. Barnes."

"Barnes, eh?"

"Hamilton Barnes! I need him."

"You know him, then?" The policeman scowled at Vi, taking in her expensive dress, shoes, and bag. "What's all this now?"

Vi explained quickly as possible and the policeman's face changed from doubtful to concerned. He took off a few minutes later, darting for the closest office with Violet and Ginny chasing after.

A call later and the policeman turned to them. "Mr. Barnes isn't in. But they know where he is. One of the boys is getting him. You're to go home if Mr. Barnes knows where that is.

Otherwise, I'll take you to the station."

"He knows where I live," Violet said. Now that she had help, the shaking was starting and

Violet stared helplessly at the policeman. "I...he's...oh goodness, he has my baby sister."

"It'll be all right," Ginny said, quoting Violet. "You know who to look for."

Violet pressed her lips together and nodded quickly.

"Let's get you home now," the policeman said.

He had one of the men in the station get a cab. When it arrived, the policeman opened the door for Violet. Ginny slipped in beside Vi and the bobby joined them. He got the address from Violet, and the drive across London was a century-long, a millennium. How would she face her father? Lady Eleanor? What if they didn't get Isolde back? What if something happened that she couldn't fix later?

They stopped in front of the house, and Violet didn't even realize she was home for a moment until the policeman got out and opened the door. As Violet was handed out, Victor and Jack came running down the stairs.

"Vi! We heard." Victor wrapped his arm around her and pulled her inside. Ginny paused, but Vi reached out and grabbed the girl's hand, pulling her along behind.

Inside the house, Vi and Ginny were taken to the parlor where they recounted the story.

"There's more than you know, darling," Victor said. "Jack missed your date because he and Barnes also realized that Hugo was the killer. Gulliver was seen storming off after the squabble with Danvers. These Yard boys were tracking Hugo down. They've got eyes on his apartment, his yacht, his business offices. He'll turn up with Isolde and we'll have them both."

Violet nodded, but her gaze was caught by the sight of Ginny staring around in wonder. The girl was amazed while Violet was dying inside. She slowly breathed in and let it out, once, twice, again, but it wasn't helping.

Jack said something, but Violet didn't hear it. She rose as though a puppet master had yanked her strings, pacing between the windows. If Jack tried to talk to her again, she didn't notice. She missed whatever was said between Ginny and the men, between the policeman and Victor. All of it.

What if she'd just gone with Isolde to look at hats? What if they'd stayed in? Isolde shouldn't have been out and about so soon. She should have been safe at home, pretending to mourn.

Finally, someone stopped her in her tracks. Vi glanced up expecting Victor, but it was Jack.

"This is not your fault."

Violet licked her lips and disagreed. "She's my baby sister. She was here because it was our job to protect her."

"No one could have guessed that Hugo Danvers would come after her."

"But we did," Violet countered. "We knew he was infatuated with her. Helen just told us that Hugo tended to be obsessive. We knew he'd pressed his attentions on her. We knew he'd shown up here to commiserate and mourn together. That wasn't right. We should have known right then that..."

"We did," Victor said. "We knew exactly that. It was *I*-not you Vi, *I* told him to never come back. To leave Isolde alone. It was one of the reasons why I was so behind the plan of Bruges. She needs to avoid the gossip, but more so—him. I was the one who took Isolde away from him. I was the one who caused this."

CHAPTER TWENTY-TWO

It had been before luncheon when Violet and Ginny returned to the house with the policeman. In a vague sort of way, Violet heard Ginny tell Victor she didn't need to worry about getting home and could stay as long as she liked. Vi would have addressed that at any other moment, but her mind was skipping over what had happened again and again.

They'd gone shopping. How had Hugo known that they'd be there?

"He must have been watching the house. If he saw the servants leave yesterday but didn't see Gerald take Isolde, then the house-breaking was the first attempt to take her with him."

Victor started and Jack slowly turned. "What now?"

"Yesterday, when we got back from our trip to Margate," Violet said. "Someone had attempted to force their way into the house. Of course, it had to be Hugo."

"Why haven't I heard of this?" Jack demanded.

"You would have heard all about it," Violet said, "if you'd

been able to come last night." Jack paused, and Violet only realized then how that must have sounded. She sighed.

"She didn't mean it like that," Victor told Jack. "She meant literally. We intended to tell you all."

Violet didn't have time for the tender feelings of men or the brainwork to waste on those feelings. Her sister had been taken. *Why?* What could he hope to gain? Unless...Violet considered, remembering that day in the parlor, just over there. He'd pressed in on Isolde, not even seeing her distress. He hadn't cared what she felt, only cared about telling her what he'd wanted her to know. What had it been? Hugo had watched Isolde since before she was old enough for him to approach her. Violet shivered at the idea of the younger Isolde having someone fixated on her.

"He is obsessed with her. Like a brain fever. He wants her to the exclusion of even how she feels. What did he call her?"

Victor shrugged, staring at Violet, and she remembered all at once.

"An angel. She isn't real to him. She's an infatuation, like being in love with Aphrodite or someone from a book. Only Isolde is something you can snatch. Something you can stalk. Lion to deer. He watched and waited and...my god, he killed his father. For what? They hated each other. His father would have been more likely to leave anything—should there have been a penny after his crimes—to a boy's school than his son. The only benefit of killing Carlton Danvers for Hugo was freeing Isolde."

"There were," Jack said, "a series of threatening letters from Hugo to Carlton. We found them yesterday. They did, in fact, refer to changing course before the wedding day."

"So he took her to keep her?" Victor asked. "He can't possibly expect to get away with his plan."

"Of course, he does. He's evil, not stupid." Violet bounced on her feet. "Of course, he has a plan."

"The yacht," Jack said. "If he wants to keep her, if he thinks he can get away with this kidnapping, it's the yacht."

"I'm coming with you," Victor and Violet said in unison. Neither of them fought with the other. Both kept their attention on Jack.

"No," Jack immediately replied, only to Violet. "It's too risky."

Victor let him direct his objections to Vi while he ordered his coat and cane.

"I'm going," Violet said, but Jack didn't even reply again. Just headed for the door while

Victor followed.

"Sorry, luv," Victor mouthed and then followed Jack down the street to the main thoroughfare where a cab could be found more easily.

"Ginny," Violet ordered, "be sneaky. Listen for the address they give."

The girl nodded, a smirk on her lips as she left. Violet ran up the stairs to Victor's office. She dug through it, looking for that monstrous folding knife. Just in case. She ran into her room, grabbed a big overcoat and slipped the knife into the pocket.

By the time she'd reached the front door, Ginny had returned. They followed the path of the gentlemen, catching a cab, and heading towards the docks where Hugo Danvers intended to escape England with Violet's sister.

When they arrived, there was no sign of anyone, and Violet wasn't sure where to go.

Ginny glanced around. "Wait here," the girl said.

She ran past a warehouse and into an alley, and it didn't take long before she came back with another grubby child who pointed out Hugo's yacht.

"Did you pay that creature?"

Ginny nodded and Violet warned, "Stay back, love."

Violet walked towards the yacht as bold as a child in a candy store. Just before she found the right boat, a hand pressed over her mouth and she was yanked against a large body. She knew the second her back pressed against his oversized bulk that it was Jack, so she didn't struggle as he carried her into the darkness.

"What do you think you're doing?" he demanded without removing his hand from her mouth. Violet waited patiently and when she was set down, she saw Victor smirking with a lifted brow.

"Getting my sister," Violet answered calmly.

Jack cursed.

"They were seen getting on the ship," Victor told her. "He had a knife and a gun, and Isolde was taken below decks. No one has approached the boat yet. They're waiting to get a few more men in position. But Hugo won't be leaving tonight with her."

"Let's sink the yacht," Violet suggested.

Jack shook his head. "You're assuming they'll flee to safety. Hugo just might be the kind of man who would rather Isolde die than be free."

Violet stared at Jack and shivered at the sheer idea. What the devil? "If he loves her..."

"If he loved her, she wouldn't have been kidnapped, terrified, and hauled away from what she loves. He'd be sending her flowers and trying to create a relationship with you two."

"What are we waiting for then?" Violet demanded.

"They're getting boats in place to ensure we can go after him if he takes off. And they're getting divers ready in case we need to go into the water after her. Then we'll try to bargain our way out. We need to be sympathetic."

Violet waited while they were arranging the last of things and everyone was in place before she slipped away. Before Jack could catch her, she'd launched herself onto the boat and called, "Hugo Danvers! Hugo Danvers, Isolde is only 18 years old. Even if you love her, you're scaring her."

The boat rocked a little and Violet didn't turn. It could have been Jack or Victor following her, or it could have been Hugo hearing her and reacting horribly. The person stepped nearer, and Violet felt the warmth of Jack. Her body reacted to him in a way that it never did to Victor.

"Hugo, you're a good man," Vi called, lying through her teeth. "You don't want to scare her. Angels shouldn't be afraid."

Slowly the hatch to below opened and Hugo pushed Isolde out in front of him.

"If you cared about her, you wouldn't have brought him," Hugo snarled.

Violet didn't turn around, but she said gently, "What could a woman like me do to stop him from coming?"

Violet let her gaze flick to Isolde. She'd bitten her lip bloody, she was whiter than a ghost, and the kohl on her eyes was black circles from weeping. Vi could see her dress was ripped. She's still wearing it, Vi told herself. By Jove, she thought, I will peel his flesh from his bones if he did more to her than tear her dress.

"She needs a protector," Violet said gently.

"That's my role," Hugo snarled. His eyes were wild, and his hair looked as though he'd been through a terrible storm. His tie was askew, and his clothes were wrinkled. The scowl on his face could have scared a devil.

"I'm sorry," Violet said. "It's all my fault. I was jealous. I could see that Isolde had made you love her and your father as well. I shouldn't have tried to get between you. I just couldn't help but wonder why her, and not me. Please let Isolde go. Please, let's be friends."

Isolde was shaking like a leaf in Hugo's hands. He kept her pressed to him with a gun in one hand. It was only then that

Violet saw the knife in his other. It was pressed against Isol-de's side, and Violet choked back a cry at the sight of blood. Had he stabbed her deeply or was that a shallow cut? The blood didn't seem to be such a large circle

"Put the knife down," Violet pled. "She's bleeding. Or just let me help her. Jack will stay back, won't you? I'll help Isolde, and you two can calm things down. We need you to protect us. To care for us. To look after us. Isolde needs you to do that, Hugo. She needs you to work things out so you can be together."

Hugo waved Violet forward but told Jack to stop. Violet could hear Jack's preparations in her mind. But she could see the blood on Isolde, and the blood in Vi's ears was pounding so it seemed as though everything was coming through the rush of that sound.

Help was coming. Isolde was bleeding. Help was coming, but was it already too late? They needed to get away from this madman. What had Jack said? Hugo might be the kind of man who'd rather see Isolde dead than free. The need to flee pounded in Violet's ears with her blood, and a horrible plan was forming.

Hugo grabbed Violet's arm as she tried to pass him. "Let me help her. Let her sister help your angel. You don't want your angel hurt. You don't want her scarred. You don't want to lose her by accident."

It was the scarred that did it. Hugo pulled Violet forward and shoved both Isolde and Violet behind him, pointing a gun at Vi to keep Jack back. Behind Hugo was closer to the railing.

How like a man to assume that a woman wouldn't rescue both herself and her sister.

Violet wrapped Isolde up in a hug as Jack and Hugo hissed orders at each other, neither giving an inch. With Isolde clutched close, Vi whispered, "Men never give women the credit they deserve."

Violet yanked on her sister, throwing them both into the drink and gunshots rang out overhead. Violet could hear two grunts of pain but the water closed over her. She kept her hand on Isolde's arm and as they surfaced, there were a series of splashes near them.

Violet glanced around, searching desperately for who had followed them in and saw Jack and Hugo fighting in the water while Victor was swimming closer. It was dark, but the moment they hit the water, torches were aimed at the water.

"Vi! Give her to me."

Violet pushed her sister in the arms of their brother. The fall must have terrified poor Isolde into a faint, or the terror had. Her eyes were wide and unseeing. She was just starting to realize she was free of Hugo.

"Steady now!" someone called. "We're coming for you. Hold tight."

Violet saw a lamp on a post and swam towards it. Victor swam next to her, tugging Isolde along. The sounds of struggling continued, but Violet didn't let herself think of it.

Then another shot rang out, and everything inside of Violet stilled.

"I got him," Hamilton Barnes called. "Are you all right, Jack?"

"Fellow pricked me. But it's not too bad," Jack said.

Violet shuddered with relief and saw that Jack's bulk turned towards her. She waited until he reached her and then they swam side-by-side towards those who'd come to rescue them. They left the darkness and the terror to pursue the light. The poetry of it was not lost on Violet, though it wasn't poetry she wanted but a bath.

So low only she could hear, Jack declared, "I'm going to wring your neck."

She glanced over and pushed her hair out of her face, treading water for a moment so she could wink at him. "You might have to get in line after my father and Gerald hear of it."

"I'll just get to you first."

Violet reached her hands up to Victor, who had already gotten into the boat. He pulled her out of the water while the oarsmen pulled out Jack.

"What's this?" Victor asked. "Threatening Vi with a good beating for jumping in the river? You should have seen it coming. You haven't been spending time with a rector's daughter who embroiders. Shouldn't expect her to act like that either."

"Is he dead?" Isolde asked. She'd let go of whatever control she had and crawled to Violet, weeping.

"He's gone," Jack said. "They'll pull his body out once we're safe."

"Thank god," Isolde said. "Oh god, Vi, thank god. Thank god he's dead."

Violet pulled Isolde close, wrapping her little sister up tightly, and Victor put a blanket around them both. They were taken to a cab, to their home, to the baths, and forced to drink hot tea and scotch until they were bursting.

A doctor came to Isolde and examined her side, but the cut hadn't been deep. She might have a bit of a scar, but it wouldn't keep her down for long.

Isolde couldn't sleep alone, so Violet put her sister into her kimono and into Violet's bed. They slept with the lights on even though Violet had become very suddenly sure that if she were in danger—or if she'd fallen into the river—or both —someone would go in after her. That warmed her far more than all the hot tea and scotch could have.

CHAPTER TWENTY-THREE

Violet woke to flowers and chocolates but no Jack. Isolde woke to the screeches of her mother, which only ended when their father literally picked up Lady Eleanor and carried her out of the room and told her to get ahold of herself.

In the end, they had a big family breakfast and plans were made far ahead of Violet's capacity to control them. It only stopped when Victor said, "We aren't going for that long. Neither Vi nor myself wish to travel the world for a year and more. I agree that Isolde needs distance and time to recover from her ordeal. You'll need to find someone to come along for the longer tour. Vi and I will be doing Belgium and that is all."

Violet's look of thanks would have to be enough as everyone turned to Victor.

"Taking your sister traveling is too much?" Lady Eleanor demanded. "After her trials?" "Yes," Victor said. "We have concerns here."

"I'll do it," Gerald said. "Halpert has the estates well in hand. He doesn't need me. With Father to step in here and there, I'll go with the young ones. When Victor and Violet are ready to come home, I'll take Isolde on the more extensive tour."

"Well," Lady Eleanor sniffed. "It isn't only Isolde who needs to consider different company," she said with an eye on Vi. "Perhaps that St. Marks fellow."

"Nothing wrong with Wakefield," Father said idly. "I say, what did you put in my coffee, Victor?"

Victor looked positively mischievous when he answered, "Chocolate liqueur."

"Oh," Father said, thinking it over. "Fill me up again, boy. That's good stuff. I hope you got me a few bottles when you were buying yours."

———

"You'll be gone how long?" Jack asked. He wore pajamas and sat, very ungraciously, in a bed in the hospital ward. His wound had gotten infected from the river water and his fevers came and went. They were gone at the moment, but the doctors wouldn't let Jack leave.

"Not as long as Isolde, but a good while," Violet replied carefully. She rearranged the pillow behind his back and handed him the box of chocolates she'd brought him. They went rather nicely with the flowers. The expression when she'd given him his very feminine gift was all that she could have wished. Humor-filled and aware of the irony.

"You'll tell me when you get back?"

Violet nodded, wanting to weep a little, but she'd given herself a good scold. Surely she hadn't fallen for this great lummox quite so quickly? Surely this wasn't love that made her chest hurt so? Surely she wasn't lying to herself to make this separation easier?

"Bruges is beautiful," Jack said. "It'll be more beautiful with you there."

He fell silent and she swallowed. They both looked up in gratitude to Victor as he entered the room as though trying to shake off a demon.

"These nurses are something else," he said. "Bring a fellow a little box of things and suddenly you're a purveyor of vice and shenanigans."

"What did you bring?" Jack asked curiously, as Victor set a wooden box on the end of his bed.

"A little of this, a little of that. The good stuff."

"The only things I will admit to helping choose is the sandwich, the chocolates, and the ginger wine," Violet declared.

"I'll take responsibility for the rest. Cigars, limoncello, grenadine, chocolate liqueur, Campari, and assurances. All but the last are the results of our recent travels. The last is because I know a man smitten when I see him, and I'll bring her back."

"Do I look like I'm endlessly zozzled?"

"Not yet, but if you keep pursuing Vi, you'll be driven to drink." Victor laughed uproariously while Violet elbowed him in the side. She rose and rearranged Jack's things, putting it all away and leaving him with a tidy piece of the hospital ward.

"I'll bring you back Vi and genever," Victor assured him. "Chin up, cheerio. It'll turn out all right in the end. A little time apart and the heart will grow fonder and all that. You know. So they say. Etcetera, etcetera."

"Very eloquent," Vi told Victor.

"One tries."

Violet pressed Jack's hand, and they were gone.

THE END

Hullo, my dahlings, hullo! You are all ab fab! Are there words enough for how much I love you for reading my books and giving me a chance? Writing books for a living is simply the bees knees! Almost as wonderful are reviews, and indie folks, like myself, need them desperately! If you wouldn't mind, I would be so grateful for a review.

The sequel to this book, *Murder at the Folly* is available now.

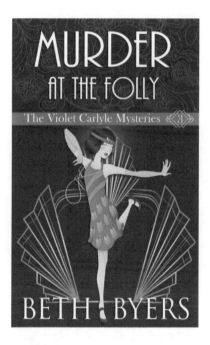

September 1923.

When Violet and Victor run into an old friend in Belgium, they have an idea of what to expect. What they don't expect is to be followed back to England, persuaded to spend an additional weekend away from home, or to have their group experience another murder.

This time, the suspect is their long-time friend Tomas

St. Marks——a shell-shocked former soldier. The race is on to discover the real killer before someone they know to be gentle and kind is taken in for a crime he didn't commit.

Order your copy here.

I am delighted to announce a new series is available for preorder now.

April 1961

Cat Clarke tends towards the naughty. You know...a little vengeful pickpocketing. A smidgeon of well-aimed fraud. A dabbling of burglary from the deserving.

She's a woman with her eye on the prize, and with her unexpected team, she might have planned her greatest heist yet.

Only while she's in the act of cutting the painting from the frame, she hears a murder.

If Cat doesn't catch the killer first, the feds may never stop chasing her. Time for her team to accomplish their greatest feat yet: find the killer, leave him gift-wrapped for the feds, and disappear into the night.

Order your copy here.

If you enjoy historical mysteries, you may enjoy, *Death by the Book*, the first in a completed series.

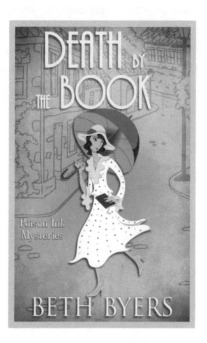

Inspired by classic fiction and Miss Buncle's Book. Death by the Book questions what happens when you throw a murder into idyllic small town England.

. . .

July 1936

When Georgette Dorothy Marsh's dividends fall along with the banks, she decides to write a book. Her only hope is to bring her account out of overdraft and possibly buy some hens. The problem is that she has so little imagination she uses her neighbors for inspiration.

She little expects anyone to realize what she's done. So when *Chronicles of Harper's Bend* becomes a bestseller, her neighbors are questing to find out just who this "Joe Johns" is and punish him.

Things escalate beyond what anyone would imagine when one of her prominent characters turns up dead. It seems that the fictional end Georgette had written for the character spurred a real-life murder. Now to find the killer before it is discovered who the author is and she becomes the next victim.

Keep on flipping to read the first chapter or order your copy here.

SNEAK PEEK OF DEATH BY THE BOOK

GEORGETTE MARSH

Georgette Dorothy Marsh stared at the statement from her bank with a dawning horror. The dividends had been falling, but this...this wasn't livable. She bit down on the inside of her lip and swallowed frantically. *What was she going to do?* Tears were burning in the back of her eyes, and her heart was racing frantically.

There wasn't enough for—for—anything. Not for cream for her tea or resoling her shoes or firewood for the winter. Georgette glanced out the window, remembered it was spring, and realized that something must be done.

Something, but *what*?

"Miss?" Eunice said from the doorway, "the tea at Mrs. Wilkes is this afternoon. You asked me to remind you."

Georgette nodded, frantically trying to hide her tears from her maid, but the servant had known Georgette since the day of her birth, caring for her from her infancy to the current day.

"What has happened?"

"The...the dividends," Georgette breathed. She didn't have enough air to speak clearly. "The dividends. It's not enough."

Eunice's head cocked as she examined her mistress and then she said, "Something must be done."

"But what?" Georgette asked, biting down on her lip again. *Hard.*

————

CHARLES AARON

"Uncle?"

Charles Aaron glanced up from the stack of papers on his desk at his nephew some weeks after Georgette Marsh had written her book in a fury of desperation. It was Robert Aaron who had discovered the book, and it was Charles Aaron who would give it life.

Robert had been working at Aaron & Luther Publishing House for a year before Georgette's book appeared in the mail, and he read the slush pile of books that were submitted by new authors before either of the partners stepped in. It was an excellent rewarding work when you found that one book that separated itself from the pile, and Robert got that thrill of excitement every time he found a book that had a touch of *something*. It was the very feeling that had Charles himself pursuing a career in publishing and eventually creating his own firm.

It didn't seem to matter that Charles had his long history of discovering authors and their books. Familiarity had most definitely *not* led to contempt. He was, he had to admit, in love with reading—fiction especially—and the creative mind. He had learned that some of the books he found would speak only to him.

Often, however, some he loved would become best sellers. With the best sellers, Charles felt he was sharing a delightful secret with the world. There was magic in discovering a new writer. A contagious sort of magic that had infected Robert. There was nothing that Charles enjoyed more than hearing someone recommend a book he'd published to another.

"You've found something?"

Robert shrugged, but he also handed the manuscript over a smile right on the edge of his lips and shining eyes that flicked to the manuscript over and over again. "Yes, I think so." He wasn't confident enough yet to feel certain, but Charles had noticed for some time that Robert was getting closer and closer to no longer needing anyone to guide him.

"I'll look it over soon."

It was the end of the day and Charles had a headache building behind his eyes. He always did on the days when he had to deal with the bestseller Thomas Spencer. He was too successful for his own good and expected any publishing company to bend entirely to his will.

Robert watched Charles load the manuscript into his satchel, bouncing just a little before he pulled back and cleared his throat. The boy—man, Charles supposed—smoothed his suit, flashed a grin, and left the office. Leaving for the day wasn't a bad plan. He took his satchel and—as usual—had dinner at his club before retiring to a corner of the room with an overstuffed armchair, an Old-Fashioned, and his pipe.

Charles glanced around the club, noting the other regulars. Most of them were bachelors who found it easier to eat at the club than to employ a cook. Every once in a while there was a family man who'd escaped the house for an evening with the gents, but for the most part—it was bachelors like himself.

When Charles opened the neat pages of 'Joseph Jones's

The Chronicles of Harper's Bend, he intended to read only a small portion of the book. To get a feel for what Robert had seen and perhaps determine whether it was worth a more thorough look. After a few pages, Charles decided upon just a few more. A few more pages after that, and he left his club to return home and finish the book by his own fire.

It might have been early summer, but they were also in the middle of a ferocious storm. Charles preferred the crackle of fire wherever possible when he read, as well as a good cup of tea. There was no question that the book was well done. There was no question that Charles would be contacting the author and making an offer on the book. *The Chronicles of Harper's Bend* was, in fact, so captivating in its honesty, he couldn't quite decide whether this author loved the small towns of England or despised them. He rather felt it might be both.

Either way, it was quietly sarcastic and so true to the little village that raised Charles Aaron that he felt he might turn the page and discover the old woman who'd lived next door to his parents or the vicar of the church he'd attended as a boy. Charles felt as though he knew the people stepping off the pages.

Yes, Charles thought, yes. This one, he thought, *this* would be a best seller. Charles could feel it in his bones. He tapped out his pipe into the ashtray. This would be one of those books he looked back on with pride at having been the first to know that this book was the next big thing. Despite the lateness of the hour, Charles approached his bedroom with an energized delight. A letter would be going out in the morning.

———

GEORGETTE MARSH

It was on the very night that Charles read the *Chronicles* that Miss Georgette Dorothy Marsh paced, once again, in front of her fireplace. The wind whipped through the town of Bard's Crook sending a flurry of leaves swirling around the graves in the small churchyard and then shooing them down to a small lane off of High Street where the elderly Mrs. Henry Parker had been awake for some time. She had woken worried over her granddaughter who was recovering too slowly from the measles.

The wind rushed through the cottages at the end of the lane, causing the gate at the Wilkes house to rattle. Dr. Wilkes and his wife were curled up together in their bed sharing warmth in the face of the changing weather. A couple much in love, snuggling into their beds on a windy evening was a joy for them both.

The leaves settled into a pile in the corner of the picket fence right at the very last cottage on that lane of Miss Georgette Dorothy Marsh. Throughout most of Bard's Crook, people were sleeping. Their hot water bottles were at the ends of their beds, their blankets were piled high, and they went to bed prepared for another day. The unseasonable chill had more than one household enjoying a warm cup of milk at bedtime, though not Miss Marsh's economizing household.

Miss Marsh, unlike the others, was not asleep. She didn't have a fire as she was quite at the end of her income and every adjustment must be made. If she were going to be honest with herself, and she very much didn't want to be—she was past the end of her income. Her account had become overdraft, her dividends had dried up, and it might be time to recognize that her last-ditch effort of writing a book about her neighbors had not been successful.

She had looked at the lives of folks like Anthony Trollope

who both worked and wrote novels and Louisa May Alcott who wrote to relieve the stress of her life and to help bring in financial help. As much as Georgette loved to read, and she did, she loved the idea that somewhere out there an author was using their art to restart their lives. There was a romance to being a writer, but she wondered just how many writers were pragmatic behind the fairytales they crafted. It wasn't, Georgette thought, going to be her story like Louisa May Alcott. Georgette was going to do something else.

"Miss Georgie," Eunice said, "I can hear you. You'll catch something dreadful if you don't sleep." The sound of muttering chased Georgie, who had little doubt Eunice was complaining about catching something dreadful herself.

"I'm sorry, Eunice," Georgie called. "I—" Georgie opened the door to her bedroom and faced the woman. She had worked for Mr. and Mrs. Marsh when Georgie had been born and in all the years of loss and change, Eunice had never left Georgie. Even now when the economies made them both uncomfortable. "Perhaps—"

"It'll be all right in the end, Miss Georgie. Now to bed with you."

Georgette did not, however, go to bed. Instead, she pulled out her pen and paper and listed all of the things she might do to further economize. They had a kitchen garden already, and it provided the vast majority of what they ate. They did their own mending and did not buy new clothes. They had one goat that they milked and made their own cheese. Though Georgette had to recognize that she rather feared goats. They were, of all creatures, devils. They would just randomly knock one over.

Georgie shivered and refused to consider further goats. Perhaps she could tutor someone? She thought about those she knew and realized that no one in Bard's Crook would hire the quiet Georgette Dorothy Marsh to influence their children. The village's wallflower and cipher? Hardly a legitimate option for any caring parent. Georgette was all too aware of what her neighbors thought of her. She rose again, pacing more quietly as she considered and rejected her options.

Georgie paced until quite late and then sat down with her pen and paper and wondered if she should try again with her writing. Something else. Something with more imagination. She had started her book with fits until she'd landed on practicing writing by describing an episode of her village. It had grown into something more, something beyond Bard's Crook with just conclusions to the lives she saw around her.

When she'd started *The Chronicles of Harper's Bend,* she had been more desperate than desirous of a career in writing. Once again, she recognized that she must do something and she wasn't well-suited to anything but writing. There were no typist jobs in Bard's Crook, no secretarial work. The time when rich men paid for companions for their wives or elderly mothers was over, and the whole of the world was struggling to survive, Georgette included.

She'd thought of going to London for work, but if she left her snug little cottage, she'd have to pay for lodging elsewhere. Georgie sighed into her palm and then went to bed. There was little else to do at that moment. Something, however, must be done.

Order your copy here.

ALSO BY BETH BYERS

THE VIOLET CARLYLE COZY HISTORICAL MYSTERIES

(This series is ongoing.)

Murder & the Heir

Murder at Kennington House

Murder at the Folly

A Merry Little Murder

Murder Among the Roses

Murder in the Shallows

Gin & Murder

Obsidian Murder

Murder at the Ladies Club

Weddings Vows & Murder

A Jazzy Little Murder

Murder by Chocolate

A Friendly Little Murder

Murder by the Sea

Murder On All Hallows

Murder in the Shadows

A Jolly Little Murder

Hijinks & Murder

Love & Murder

A Zestful Little Murder

A Murder Most Odd

Nearly A Murder

A Treasured Little Murder

A Cozy Little Murder

Masked Murderer

Meddlesome Madness: A short story collection

Silver Bells & Murder

Murder at Midnight

A Fabulous Little Murder

Murder On a Yacht

Murder On the Boardwalk (coming soon)

THE MYSTERIES OF SEVERINE DUNOIR

(This series is ongoing.)

The Mystery at the Edge of Madness

The Mysterious Point of Deceit

Mystery in the Darkest Shadow

The Wicked Fringe of Mystery

The Lurid Possibility of Murder

The Uncountable Price of Mystery

The Inexorable Tide of Mystery

The Unexpected Flavor of Forever (coming soon)

THE CAT CLARKE MYSTERIES

****A New Series****

Stealing Murder

THE POISON INK MYSTERIES

(This series is complete.)

Death By the Book

Death Witnessed

Death by Blackmail

Death Misconstrued

Deathly Ever After

Death in the Mirror

A Merry Little Death

Death Between the Pages

Death in the Beginning

A Lonely Little Death

THE 2ND CHANCE DINER MYSTERIES

(This series is complete.)

Spaghetti, Meatballs, & Murder

Cookies & Catastrophe

Poison & Pie

Double Mocha Murder

Cinnamon Rolls & Cyanide

Tea & Temptation

Donuts & Danger

Scones & Scandal

Lemonade & Loathing

Wedding Cake & Woe

Honeymoons & Honeydew

The Pumpkin Problem

THE HETTIE & RO ADVENTURES

cowritten with Bettie Jane

(This series is complete.)

Philanderer Gone

Adventurer Gone

Holiday Gone

Aeronaut Gone

Made in United States
Troutdale, OR
09/09/2023

12766252R00130